the PERSONA

GREEN-FLESHED FIENDS

AIRSHIP 27 PRODUCTIONS

The Persona
"Green-Fleshed Fiends" © 2019 Michael F. Housel

Published by Airship 27 Productions
www.airship27.com
www.airship27hangar.com

Interior illustrations © 2019 Kevin Broden
Cover illustration © 2019 Chris Rawding

Editor: Ron Fortier
Associate Editor: Fred Adams Jr.
Marketing and Promotions Manager: Michael Vance
Production and design by Rob Davis.

ISBN-13: 978-1-946183-64-4

Printed in the United States of America

10 9 8 7 6 5 4 3 2 1

GREEN-FLESHED FIENDS
by
Michael F. Housel

PROLOGUE

To: Miss Stacey Standish   June 3, 1939
Spinster's Boarding Home for Women
729 W. Rebound Ave.
2nd Floor, Room Y
Brink Town, NJ 08739

Dear Miss Stacey Standish:

Allow me to introduce myself; my name is Melody Montorto. I am president of the local branch of Specialized Insight Investigational Services (SIIS), which is located along the outskirts of Brink Town, in a farmland stretch west of Camden.

It was my hope to reach Mister Michael Mansford directly, to whom I have sent several correspondences, but to date have received no response. I can only assume that my letters have been discarded by his staff, and as such, I now reach out to you, Miss Standish, for the sake of establishing contact. (I should also mention that my early attempts to meet Mr. Mansford face-to-face proved most frustrating, due to the stringent protocol implemented at the various social events he attends.)

In any event, I know you are Mister Mansford's confidant, and in a more significant way than the Brink Town Time's Society Page dares convey. In this regard, I know that you are familiar with Mr. Mansford's alter-ego, the Persona, whose presence (I intuitively detect) yet thrives within the depths of your subconscious and on occasion, even during your cognitive modes. Be assured that whether you find my disclosure truthful or absurd, it must be presented to Mister Mansford and without caution or concern, for I have no intention of revealing his identity, or your special relationship to him, to Brink Town's citizenry, even though most of its members likely suspect such a link. I only mention such to demonstrate my unique insight, in hopes it may ensure Mister Mansford's assistance in this matter of utmost urgency.

I must secondly confess, that my home is, in fact, the SIIS headquarters, near which various atmospheric vibrations have grown most acute. It was during early spring, in particular, that I began to discern a startlingly high rise in paranormal activity within the varying vegetated patches across the field from my abode and with such, the appearance of small specimens, whose features are, I dare say, rather akin to those of goblins, leprechauns or trolls. (I know such may sound ridiculous on the surface, but please do believe me when I state my claim is legitimate.)

The creatures' manifestation would not necessarily be reason for alarm (for I am aware such entities do make their way into our dimension on occasion), but I have come to learn that they are on a desperate exodus from an opposing force that has invaded their indigenous base: a dimension, from what I can unravel, is stationed right outside our own.

It appears that only through an inadvertent, inter-dimensional rift have these entities achieved temporary sanctuary from their aggressors—but make no mistake, the marauders (who are far larger and stronger than those with whom I have thus far conversed) will also find their way into our world.

I am confident that if Mister Mansford ruminates upon this matter (and he should have no problem doing so via his extrasensory abilities), he would acknowledge the gravity of the situation and lend to it his investigational support.

Please, Miss Standish, I implore you to share this information with Mister Mansford and ask that he please phone me at his earliest convenience at FAUXFIELD-7105. (I will be available around the clock.) He has nothing to lose in so doing, and from that point, if he so graciously consents; I will give him directions to my home and escort him directly to the occupied area.

Thank you (and Mister Mansford) for your time and consideration on this most pressing concern.

Sincerely,

Miss Melody Montorto,
President, SIIS/Brink Town, NJ

I

Standish tapped her foot, anxious for the meeting to end. She heard some murmurings within, some shuffling of paper and then as the knob turned laughter.

"That's the best one yet," blurted old Carl Clive, editor of the Brink Town Times, shaking his head and as he stepped out. "Always the comedian, Mike." He glanced into the hall and caught Standish's eye. "Well, what a pleasant sight." He turned back and hollered. "Say, Mike, the love of your life's here. Why don't you pull that little stunt on her? See what she thinks."

She glanced at Mansford, who fiddled with a writhing, rattling green snake—shiny and fake—just as a brown-tinged counterpart bristled from out his vest and coiled down onto the conference table.

The men standing about the table pointed and laughed.

Mansford's right-hand man, Ned Stark, scooped the snake up by the neck and spun it into his vest pocket. He then reached over and snatched the other from Mansford's fumbling fingers and pocketed it as well.

"They'll sell like hotcakes," Ned said, making certain Carl heard. "Remember, now, do right by us—full-page ads, six weeks before Halloween, with the usual discount."

"Sure," Clive chuckled. "I always ensure a long run for any of the crazy stuff you supply and all for a reasonable fee. Really, Ned, when have I let you down?"

"Never," Mansford interjected before Stark could reply. "You always come through, Carl."

The confirmation resulted in a strange, mute exchange, wherein Clive and Mansford held each other's gaze. Clive looked to Stark, and the two then adapted a similar link, expanding the unspoken, mystical alignment.

Mansford, of course, was cognitive of what had transpired among them: how his friends—most of Brink Town, in fact—had teamed with the Persona to defeat the Great Beguiler and his evil minions. He also knew that Clive and Stark harbored memories of the event, but now such recollections had dulled to mere dream-like fragments. It had to be that way, or so Saint Peter (ersatz, the smoky-faced Surrogate) had said, yet for the life of him, Mansford (though respectful of his alter-ego's influence) never understood why.

"Sure...sure, I always come through," Clive croaked, blinking hard to snap his stupor. "I mean, it's mutual, after all. One hand washes the other, right?"

The onlookers smiled and nodded before bidding goodbye, sidestepping their seats to spin Clive around as they flooded outward, ushering him toward

Standish, who raised a delicate hand and placed it upon his back.

Clive turned and looked at her, so that they, too, formed a lingering link, which acknowledged they were of the same league, designed to fight in the same crusade, whatever it might be.

Clive smiled, breaking the link, allowing Standish to charge into the office, as she received several admiring glances from the men yet exiting. It was understandable. Even in her dowdy, attire, she still conjured thoughts of the late, great Harlow.

Mansford greeted her with a wink, and Stark waved her nearer, their eyes locking, triggering another intuitive exchange.

Stark held it for a moment, but then glanced away. "Mike made a good impression today," he bleeped. "Got ourselves some serious backers, I believe." He fingered the green tail that protruded from his pocket and tucked it back in, prompting a muffled rattle as he marched toward the door." This gag could prove our most profitable to date."

"I'm happy for you, Ned," Standish chirped, opening her purse to extract an envelope. "Michael told me you worked hard on the prototype."

"Well, the prototype is always most important," he explained. "You know what they say about first impressions…" Grinning, he then shot the couple a curt salute and continued into the hall. "I'll get crackin' on those contracts. Chat with you love birds later."

Standish waited until Stark's meandered from sight and handed the envelope to Mansford giving him a suspicious shrug, as if to say he harbored something he had not yet confessed.

He grinned and shrugged back, but after a moment, his expression grew grim. "I take it, this is important." He held the envelope to the light, waving the opened end like a fan, while pointing behind her. "Close the door, would you, dear?"

Standish complied and walked back with arms folded, impatient for him to extract the letter. "Well, are you going to read it?"

With a sturdy snap, he removed the paper and unfolded it. "Oh, my," he said with a curious scan, "indeed, I've not received any prior correspondence to this, but as you well know, the gals in the mailroom generally sift through the crackpot stuff. I—the Persona? Really, now, how silly."

"And I, your confidant, who stores your identity within her subconscious," Standish added. "Equally silly."

"Indeed," Mansford concurred. "Utterly preposterous."

There was something in his quip that angered her. "I dream about it," she confessed, and her eyes misted. "I dream about it all the time, in fact. I dream about my parents…their disappearance…their whereabouts. I dream of the Ministry of Chaotic Command—the accursed name weighing on my brain, and I don't even know why. These things linger…influence me…well beyond my sleep. They were on my mind when I gave you the white scarf. I had envisioned your wearing it, Michael…envisioned you soaring down the street…the scarf spiraling around your neck so gallantly…the flaps of your Edwardian jacket billowing…that pearly mask gripped to your face, and…"

Mansford bristled, though he had long suspected a revelation of this sort would surface someday. "We all dream," he replied. "That doesn't mean the content of our dreams is real, that such holds any truth."

"Oh, but I say it does," Standish countered. "Dreams always hold meaning. Dreams always hold truth, and now out of the blue, a woman sends this letter, and I feel that my suspicions are confirmed. I don't care what you say, Michael. I'm certain this is more than mere coincidence."

Mansford sighed and looked again at the letter. "Strange stuff for sure," he continued, nurturing a cool facade, "but it doesn't mean she's right. These self-proclaimed psychics are often little more than con artists, or sadly, sick or delusional. This Montorto gal may have connected me to the Persona simply based on my status, assuming I was like those avenging, well-to-do chaps on the radio. She may have even spotted the photos of us on Clive's high-society page, fixed her theory for whatever odd reason and then detailed it into this cryptic correspondence." He laughed. "And as far as these tiny people go, wouldn't you think I'd have caught wind of such if I were, in fact, Brink Town's exalted crusader?"

"I suppose," she murmured. "Though I must say, the Persona doesn't seem inclined to wander beyond Brink Town. Maybe you simply haven't had time to scope anything beyond the immediate vicinity."

"Okay," Mansford relented with a grin. "Think what you will, my dear." He drummed his jaw. "Tell you what. For the fun of it, I'll call this Miss Montorto, schedule a visit and see if I can get down to the nitty-gritty. If she's a kook, I'll be nice and humor her, but if she's planning some misguided blackmail stunt, I'll threaten to take her to the authorities. Either way, the air will be cleared."

Standish pouted. "I wish you wouldn't be so presumptuous, Michael." She again recalled her dreams and their uncanny depth. "I mean, what if there is something to what she claims? Really, what then?"

Mansford rolled his eyes and fanned the letter. "I'll take Jack Murphy and Phil Sutton along. I'll make sure Jack wears his police uniform for the authoritative factor, and Phil…well, you know how shrewd Phil is. Nonetheless, I bet you nine-out-of-ten, Miss Montorto is a withered, old bag on the cusp of senility. Besides, who else would coin such a ridiculously pretentious label—Specialized Insight Investigational Services?" He clicked his tongue "Good grief."

"I must admit," Standish confessed, "I've certainly never heard of it, and I've lived here my whole life." She sighed. "Granted, it does sound rather hokey. It's also peculiar there's no return address on the envelope. Heck, it's not even typed on the letter."

"That ought to tell you something, my sweet. In any event, don't worry your pretty head over it. I'll take it from here." He led her toward the door. "I assure you, the matter will be handled discreetly, and when all's said and done, you'll have no further contact with the mysterious Miss Montorto." He tapped her brow with the letter, smiled and opened the door. "Sound good?"

"Yes," she said, stepping out. "It's just that…"

"What, dear?"

She looked into his eyes, and if only for a fleeting moment, believed she saw her convictions solidified within his twinkling orbs—the hint of the mask, the sweeping scarf—but then dismissed the fancy. Indeed, it was foolish to think such an outlandish thing.

"It's nothing, Michael. I'll call you tonight, all right?"

"I'll be counting on it," he said and watched her shimmy down the hall. He then shut the door and with great haste, reread the letter.

This time he savored the words, finding neither deceit nor insincerity in its phrasing. In fact, beneath the sentences' surface, he believed danger ooze. This unnerved the mortal part of him, but when it came to the Persona, he was obligated to intervene.

II

"So, she's nuts," Sutton said, as Mansford's Packard rolled down the country road, "and you want to use your influence to have this old dame committed."

"I never said that, Phil," Mansford answered. "Personally, I don't know what to expect at this point. Jack wasn't able to find much information on her."

"True," Murphy confirmed from the rear. "She's a vague one, all right. I wonder how long she's been in the area, though the house has been the family for several decades, passed on from uncle to aunt, niece to nephew and back again. No one stays long enough to plant roots."

"She sounded lucid enough over the phone," Mansford said, turning onto a long, bumpy, dirt pass, "not like one who'd compose such a correspondence, anyway."

"Creatures, eh?" Sutton muttered, the words rolling off his tongue with vehemence, for he recalled, if only through a subconscious burp, the Great Beguiler and his hideous legion swarming. "Creatures are never a good thing."

"I concur," said Murphy. "The idea does sound…well, unsettling, to say the least." He cleared his throat. "She claims they're small, you say, Mike?"

"Yes," Mansford said, as an ominous, gray mansion came into view. "That's the claim—and green, or so she told me over the phone. Of course, there's no need to get nervous about it." He paused and then fibbed "I'm confident they're the result of an overactive imagination."

Sutton chuckled. "Sure, what else would they be? Poor, old dame…"

Mansford parked about twenty feet from the house, its crinkled shingles and dilapidated porch projecting an unwelcoming aura.

"Well, here we are, gentlemen." Mansford flung open the door and slipped out. "Now, I'll introduce you, all right? She'll notice you're an officer, of course, Jack, but we won't make a big thing of it. You fellows just say hello, go through the basic niceties if you wish, but I'll steer the conversation."

The men nodded and exited. Mansford stretched, then smoothed his overcoat.

"Kind of warm for that," Sutton remarked, "don't you think?"

Mansford shrugged. "I like to maintain a stately image. First impressions, you know…"

"In other words," Sutton teased, "dazzle them with the old Mansford charm. Yeah, I know how it works."

Mansford pointed to the porch. "How about we cut the chit-chat and get down to business?"

"All right," Sutton grumbled, "whatever you say, boss."

The three made their way up, the boards creaking with each shaky step.

"You ought to report this to Mayor Percy," Sutton remarked. "This dive's ready to crumble—should be condemned."

Mansford ignored him and reached to the side of the oak door, his finger hovering over the bell. "Remember, be polite."

He pressed the button: a long, dull, echoing gong. A few seconds of silence followed, prompting Mansford to press again.

"Maybe she's hard of hearing," Sutton conjectured. "It's common when one reaches a certain—"

There then came the sound of an unlatching chain. The old, brass knob turned; the door creaked open.

Within a dim curve of light, a tall, long-haired beauty stood, with piercing green eyes, her face symmetrical and smooth, much like a movie star's. Her dress (if one could call it that) was dark, but sheer, her bra and panties visible beneath the thin fabric, her long, nyloned legs propped by shiny stilettos She sported a short, black cape, peaked by a high, blood-red collar.

"Appears we got the wrong place," Sutton said to her, "but please give our regards to Mister Lugosi."

Mansford shot him a disapproving glance, smiled at her and offered his hand. "Hello, I'm Michael Mansford. I'm here to see Miss Montorto." For a moment, her piercing pupils made him pause. "Is…is she at home?"

The beautiful woman took his hand, but did not shake, giving his fingertips a slight but unreadable caress, before letting go.

"Indeed, she is." Her crimson lips curled. "I'm Miss Montorto. I'm so happy you've come, Mister Mansford." She stepped to the side and gestured the men inward, giving Murphy a suspicious once-over. "Please, do come in."

"Thank you," Mansford gushed, stepping around her shapely form and into the stuffy alcove. "I hope you don't mind that I've brought along a couple colleagues. Mister Philip Sutton and Officer Jack Murphy." He cleared his throat to numb the ensuing lie. "We have a business meeting afterwards, so I thought out of convenience…"

Montorto closed the door and re-latched its rusty chain, more out of habit, Mansford assumed, than necessity.

"That's fine." Her breasts heaved with pronounced distinction. "I've no problem with additional guests, but I'm rather disappointed that Miss Standish didn't come." Her emerald eyes exuded betrayal. "When we spoke, I truly sensed it would be the three of us, granting one another intuitive support."

"Miss Standish had to work," Mansford again lied. "She'd have come otherwise."

Montorto pushed past them. "Yes, of course." Her florid perfume teased their nostrils, her sumptuous derriere shifting below the cape's fringe, as they eagerly followed. "The Brink Town Theater has a matinee today. Miss Standish would be working the ticket booth, naturally."

"An astute deduction," said Mansford, giving Murphy a sly glance, while Sutton continued to absorb her suggestive gait.

"My overall knowledge is astute," Montorto added, "which, of course, is why I asked you here."

The acknowledgement troubled Mansford, but as of yet, he was unable to read the extent of her intent and so resigned to playing along.

She led them to a drab kitchen, where strewn atop the dining table were several black-and-white photographs. She pointed to them with an air of pride. "I have documentation for you. I believe you'll find it authentic. Please sit and allow me to get you some wine."

"We'll pass," Mansford replied with unintended bluntness. "I'm a bit confused. I thought you were going to show me the real thing, Miss Montorto. Photographs can be doctored, after all."

"I offer these images," she explained, her posture calm and assured, "to give you a taste of what will come: a warm-up, if you will." She folded her arms and rolled her eyes at the table. "Well, go on. Have a look."

Mansford shook his head and gestured his friends to sit. He then leafed through the photos, most of which were murky and seemed to feature only thick patches of vegetation. However, upon closer scrutiny, he discerned within these impetuous clusters what appeared to be little, helmeted heads, around the size of a baseball. He traced the forms and from there noticed the hazy hint of hooked noses and beady eyes.

Manford handed the photographs to Murphy and Sutton, who gave them a casual view, restraining their snickers, then handed them back.

"For all I know," Mansford assessed, spreading the photos onto the table, "those figures could be dolls. With all due respect, I'm not so gullible to believe—"

"Don't play me for a fool," Montorto seethed, raising her hands. "I didn't call you here to be so callously dismissed. I'm aware of your perceptive powers. You can see through things—see the truth in them. Any layman would reject those entities as fake, but a man of sparked intellect…oh, he would know otherwise."

"Then I'm obviously not your man," Mansford concluded and looked to his friends. "Perhaps, gentlemen, it's best we left."

Montorto looked startled. "No, please," she begged, grabbing his arm as he rose. "You've come all this way, and well, I'll show you—show you where the entities hide. You'll see them living, breathing, roaming about the field. You can speak to their leader, in fact—yes, their leader, Mister Mansford." Her expression grew anxious, her breathing heavy. "I told him you were coming. He's not at all shy, quite willing to chat…to share."

Mansford had to admit, there was something enticing in Montorto's desperation, a suggestive implication in her need to convince him. Also, it did not hurt that her scent seemed to grow more inebriating by the minute.

"All right," Mansford consented, giving his friends a sly glance." You take us to these…uh, entities. I'm more than glad to converse with their leader…if he's willing, as you say."

"Oh, yes," she exclaimed, "he's willing—most willing, indeed." With child-like fervor, she pulled Mansford's hand, leading him from the kitchen. "Come... come see."

Murphy and Sutton shrugged and followed the two to the front door, which Montorto unlatched with haste and upon stepping onto the porch, locked the door behind her with a slim skeleton key, which she promptly pulled from her bosom, clicking it from right to left several times, until satisfied with its security.

She then waved them onward, down the porch, past the Packard, travelling westward into the high grass.

"They roam at the field's fringe," she said, letting go of Mansford's hand and sprinting ahead, "just before the pines. If you look downward, you'll see them shuffling."

Montorto waved the men farther into the area and then jumped in such a way to make her svelte frame all the more enticing.

"There, there," she insisted, pointing to a wavering patch. She hunkered and cooed, "Come now...don't be afraid. I'm here with Mister Mansford...yes, Mister Michael Mansford, just as I promised. That's right—go tell Sontar. Tell Sontar. Tell him Mister Mansford's here."

Sutton circled his finger around his ear, making Murphy choke back a laugh. Mansford, however, proceeded toward her, knelt and with as much compassion as he could muster, met her eager gaze.

"Sontar, you say?" he whispered. "Sounds like a barbarian name, or perhaps that of a planet in some science-fiction tale." He scanned the grass, focusing on each breeze-tussled patch. "So, you see them... How many might there be, Miss Montorto?"

She grew perturbed and thrust her finger outward. "Look, Mister Mansford—look. The answer lies right before your very eyes."

The air grew thick and tense. Mansford felt his heart steady, his pulse slow. The sensation was unlike any he had experienced before: not at all the sort of push he might have felt when absorbing someone's bad deed, but rather a throbbing, surreal anticipation, much of which seeped from out Montorto's perfumed aura, immersing him and his friends into her strange reality.

To project an unflustered stance, Mansford sharpened his focus, and it was then that he witnessed several small heads popping up from the grass, adorned by silvery, creased helmets, just as he had seen in the photos. Now that he thought of it, the entities looked like miniature conquistadors, but with green skin and hooked noses, adorned by lopsided eyebrows, curly mustaches and devilish goatees.

"Well, I'll be," he murmured.

The little men crept forth, their shiny, little swords swiping through the grass.

Uncertain whether the creatures were friend or foe, Mansford's instincts took over. His hands slipped into his pockets, into his gloves. With a curt shake, he shed his outer coat and rose in his Edwardian jacket. His white scarf curled around his neck, as his "holsters" snapped, springing forth his Punjabi dagger and onto his face, the pearly mask.

Murphy and Sutton froze, recognizing the Persona and the inundating memories that accompanied his presence, if only through a momentary spurt.

With a nudge of her mind, Montorto's acknowledged his presence as well, and encouraged him to greet the little creatures, but for the moment, the Persona held his ground.

The tiny men also paused, alarmed by the specter's shimmering countenance, their brown-sacked bodies blending back into the grass, with only one remaining.

He was a tad taller than the others, though perhaps only due to the extra height of his helmet. Also, unlike the others, his gangling frame was cloaked by a purple smock and matching cape, insinuating royalty. Even his sword appeared more fanciful than those of the others, its hilt wide and curled.

The creature's thin lips parted, creating a small, dark oval, through which he squeaked, "You are...Mansford." The creature then smacked his lips, squinted and rephrased, "No—not Mansford...it is, Persona...*the* Persona." He pumped out his chest. "Indeed, I know who you are."

Perhaps this acknowledgment should have delighted the Persona, but he could not shake an element of deceit within the creature's pompous stance and also considered the possibility that the thing and Montorto held a symbiotic link. To be certain, he wished to absorb the creature's thoughts, ascertain its background, but despite his focus, no depth or distinctions surfaced, and so with nothing further to ruminate or explore, the specter opted for a more basic tactic.

"And I," the Persona proclaimed, "know who you are, Sontar, King of the Craven." With this denouncement, the Persona's pearly sheen turned doughy and mean, his lips stretching into a wicked smirk. "Tell me, does your kind generally take delight in running from a fight?"

The creature's face contorted in offense. "You are wrong, Persona. I'll have you know, we are a proud, combative breed and only occupy your dimensional sector to garner time...and to devise a strategy." His beady eyes gleamed. "Is it not the same of those of your world, when it comes to confrontations across enemy lines?"

Sontar made a valid point and intrigued, the Persona glided closer. "Perhaps I've been a tad hasty." His expression softened. "Tell me, from where do you hail, and how is it you know the native language?

"How?" asked the creature, his eyes bouncing upon Montortoto. "Why, English has been but a dormant language within me, but I sharpened my skills through the lovely lady." He gave her a respectful nod. "She allowed me to read her mind, and in turn, I shared with her the details of our plight." He stretched a bony finger upward and pointed at the Persona's brow. "Perhaps, you wouldn't be so cruel, if you'd be so kind to reciprocate."

The Persona sensed Montorto's piercing gaze, her creased lips conveying awe and hope, and throughout it all, her encouragement continued to flow, urging him to penetrate Sontar's mind. The Persona had no objections, of course, if such could, in fact, be achieved, but if it were to occur, it had to be on his terms alone. Montorto could only at best accompany the ride.

Then to everyone's dismay, the Persona snapped the dagger back into its pouch and from the pit of his palm, triggered a magnetic surge that made the creature ascend and then hover mere inches from his scrutinizing face.

"What…what is this?" Sontar implored, flailing as his companions scurried about the grass, their panicked motions as jerky as those of Stark's fabricated snakes. "Put me down. Put me down, Persona."

"Be at ease," the Persona commanded, his tone rich and resonating. "You offered to share your thoughts, and so I have accepted your offer, though it's likely to differ from what you and the young lady shared."

In defiance, Sontar writhed, turning upside down, wobbling from side to side, kicking his boot-buckled feet. However, he soon realized the uselessness of his struggle and with a huff, managed to flip himself back up, aligning his gaze with those beneath the pliable mask.

"*That's good, little man,*" the Persona relayed, feeling Montorto's vibes intermingling with his, while keeping Murphy and Sutton's at bay. "*Open your mind. Show me what I need. Make me believe in you, as you believe in me.*"

In a vicious snap, a crackling, white sphere filled the Persona's consciousness, and within its heart, he perceived a grassy field, arched by a bright, blue sky. Little, green men marched across the expanse, Sontar directing them with a Seven Dwarfs swagger, their collective faces wrought with courage and concern.

A guttural, reverberating horn blew in the distance, causing Sontar and his band to halt. They jutted their swords, hunkered and trembled.

With this, the Persona plunged even deeper and felt the vision's atmosphere solidify and just as fast implode, blistering with fear and doom, before the

"Put me down, Persona."

ground began to rumble. Something large approached. The Persona saw—felt—Sontar crouch ever lower, anticipating his demise, while his followers scattered, leaping behind trees and rocks, watching the nearing shadows stretch and spread.

"No—no more," Sontar begged. "I...I cannot take anymore. Please—please release your hold, Persona. Let me go. Let me be. Let me not relive this horrid memory."

Though the Persona's face crackled and blurred, compelled to consume more, compassion overcame him (and an underlying sense that forcing the matter would only prove futile). He then broke the reverie, letting Sontar descend like a feather back to ground.

Murphy and Sutton rubbed their eyes, and with dazed concern, Montorto edged closer.

"There was more yet to reveal," she seethed, glancing at both the Persona and the diminutive king. "You may have seen what caused his fear—even the way the portal formed, the way it burnt through the air, granting them entrance to our world."

"I saw enough," the Persona replied, his patience waning, which in turn caused the wind to twist and circle, flattening his scarf. He tucked his gloves into his pockets. His mask dropped from his face, into its cushioned, hip compartment.

Mansford looked calm, assured. "It all looked clear enough," he said, "felt real enough." He glanced at Sontar. "So, beyond swapping thoughts with Miss Montorto, how are you managing in this new realm, and when do you anticipate returning to your own?"

Sontar seemed taken aback by Mansford's nonchalant alteration and rubbed his chin. "Your guess is as good as mine, sir. Perhaps we will forge our way through yet another dimension, if such is required. I do believe there are many pockets into which we may pass, all of them in anticipatory flux." He smirked, seeming to relish his smugness. "Still, we must remain diligent... and take our time. We need a sturdy strategy if we are to advance an attack." He cocked his sword at Montorto. "The lovely lady said you...or rather the Persona...might assist in this regard, but perhaps she was presumptuous."

"Of course, he'll help," Montorto scolded, "but you must be as open to him as you were to me. If you and your army continue to dilly-dally, all will be for naught."

"No need to jump the gun," Mansford said. "Let me converse with him in my own, individual way. He can share as he sees fit. I'll assess the facts, and then we'll see if I—or more precisely, the Persona—can be of service."

Mansford then turned to Sontar and noticed that he and his band had scampered off, with only the shuffling grass insinuating their whereabouts.

Sutton rubbed his eyes. "All right," he yawned, "what's the deal here? I don't see a damn thing."

"Yeah," groaned the drowsy Murphy, lifting his cap and rubbing his crown. "You, uh, spot anything yet, Mike?"

Mansford looked at Montorto, whose eyes begged his silence. "Not a thing, Jack."

"It appears," Montorto muttered, "that I've wasted your time. It appears I was mistaken. There're no little people here...at least not at the moment. Perhaps if you were to return some other time..."

Mansford sighed and to his friends said, "If you gents don't mind, I'd like a moment alone with Miss Montorto. I'll meet you back at the car."

Murphy and Sutton consented, though before shuffling off, gave their friend's garb a suspicious glance.

Montorto smiled, but otherwise her demeanor conveyed uncertainty.

"Take heed, Miss Montorto," he whispered. "I intend to scrutinize this matter to the fullest, but with no with guarantees. If you push me—or reach out again to Miss Standish—I swear, I will push back—and hard. You possess remarkable intuition, granted, but it's no match for mine." He reached over and lifted a silky strand off her shoulder, causing her to quiver, and then tugged it just enough to make her wince. "Have I made myself clear?"

She felt the brunt of his conviction and glanced away, though a trace of a smile remained on her lips, the cause of which he could not discern, but decided it best to let such be and gave the field a long, shrewd scan, aware Sontar and his cohorts were watching, waiting. He then sauntered away, but not before grabbing his outer coat off the ground and assuring her, "I'll be in touch...soon."

He moved with confidence, but was, in fact, perplexed by what he had encountered.

He had to research it, or at least talk to someone who might better understand its dynamics and knew precisely who fit the bill.

III

Mansford absorbed the chamber's soothing, eclectic aura: the horror-movie posters, ventriloquist dummies, curvaceous statues and above all, the mask, which he had propped upon his desk against a stack of mythology texts. Its twinkling, ethereal sheen spoke to him, quieting and unnerving him at the same time. In the process, it also unhinged his thoughts, extending them into prayer.

"Hello, Michael." Surrogate's voice entered like an echo. "I came as soon as I could." His dark, robed frame manifested as his smoke-blown face came into view, only then to reveal the bearded Saint Peter. "What's brewing, old sport?"

"I assumed you already knew."

"You always assume that," said the saint. "I have so much on my plate, so much tossed my way, that it's often hard to keep my agenda straight."

Mansford ignored the excuse and replied, "The vibrations were strong." He pointed to the mask. "I experienced a lot, but none of it felt truly right."

The saint sauntered toward the mask and grazed it. "Most curious," he remarked, his eyes rolling upward. "Green, no less."

"Yes, and evidently from another dimension," added Mansford. "The question is, how exactly did they get here? Even those little creatures don't fully understand."

"And your attractive escort?"

"Miss Montorto? Oh, she didn't elaborate much. Whatever she and the little friend shared seems convoluted, and as much as the young lady wants me to understand, I already know the matter is rather fruitless as it stands. I need direction on this, Surrogate. I know I always ask for such, and you always evade my requests, but I believe an exception is due this time."

"Alas, I've no more information than you," Saint Peter answered with predictable haste, still absorbing the mask's vibrations. "For now, I suggest you ruminate on your strange encounter, weigh its pros and cons." He spun around and smiled. "For what it's worth, you might consider returning to the source."

"Probing an inter-dimensional rift seems dangerous, if that's what you're suggesting. What if I interfere in such a way to worsen matters?"

"Worsen?" the saint quipped. "Well, you won't know until you try."

"What if these creatures prove infectious or their aggressors turn aggressive toward us?"

"If the wee ones were infectious, the consequences of such would already be apparent. As for their aggressors…well, if they're aggressive, then I'd imagine they'd be so inclined as such with anyone."

Mansford shook his head. "You're not helping."

The saint smiled. "As you well know, enlightenment never comes without a hitch in our line of work." Puffs of smoke resumed about his cheeks. "We can only conjure our courage and pray the outcomes are blessed."

"In other words," Mansford moaned, "play the game, even if the rules are fixed."

"Well put," the saint chimed and rose off the floor.

"Leaving so soon?" Mansford asked with an indignant sigh.

"I must," the saint replied. "The problems of this world never wait, and yours are but one cluster among many." He glided toward the window and paused at the ledge. "Remember, Michael, evil grows stronger whenever we hesitate. You'd be best to put your intuitive skills to work, and as I said, return to the source. That's all I can offer, Michael—the source."

He gave a humble wave and in a flash was gone, a fading blur within the declining clouds.

Mansford threw up his arms and in exasperation stomped toward the mask and lifted it. "So, what can you tell me, my faithful disguise? Come now, give me a hint."

Mansford concentrated, absorbing its subtle vibrations, his fingertips tingling. It began to glow, its sheen becoming as smooth and creamy as Montorto's skin, its contour comely...female. He recalled her inebriating perfume and grinned.

"So," he deduced, "I was mistaken. The vixen really knows more than I detected...but of course, why wouldn't she?" He propped the mask again against the texts and watched it resume its regular mode. "I shouldn't have been so hasty...should have let some trust form between us." He glanced at the phone. "Perhaps I should reestablish communication, make amends, but something tells me..."

The phone rang, just as he knew it would.

He picked up the receiver. "Yes?"

"Mister Mansford," the familiar female voice stated. He knew who it was, of course.

"Yes, this is Michael Mansford," he confirmed, playing along.

There came a pause, followed by a giggle and a strange, rhythmic admittance: "I...I hope you don't mind, but I drew your number from out of the sky. It came to me so clearly and so suddenly that I couldn't help but try..."

"Very poetic, Miss Montorto," Mansford said, "but as I recall, I said I'd be in touch—"

"I know what you said," she cooed, "but I entered a trance and honestly didn't expect much success. Pardon my boldness, but for whatever odd reason, I knew you needed me." She giggled again, but then cleared her throat and continued with marked earnestness. "If I had only managed this feat sooner, I'd not have sent those letters, particularly the last one to Miss Standish. Still, at this point, what does it matter? One must try whatever avenues are available under urgent circumstances. Hell, direct telepathy would have been the ultimate means, but then perhaps it would have been too abrupt, inadvertently caused more confusion. The thing is, now that we're in contact, and I dare say, in a most special way, I do hope you'll accept my apology. We got off on a shaky start, and it sure would be nice..."

"Yes, Miss Montorto," Mansford agreed, "a shaky start, and I do believe I must take the brunt of the blame. Sorry, too, I tugged your hair the way I did."

"I didn't mind," she confessed, "but perhaps there's a way you could make it up to me, nonetheless." There was a pause, graced by her tremulous breath. "Might we meet again, but this time just the two of us, beyond my home, beyond the field...somewhere pleasant but neutral...where our impulses might flow accordingly?"

Impulses, Mansford mused. Sounded suggestive, not the sort of thing he should leap into, and yet...

"Perhaps, Miss Montorto," he said with some hesitation, "though I'd still like to get a better grasp on the matter, before we might—"

"But I'm the one you need," she interjected. "You can look high and low, but you'll never find one like me, Mister Mansford, certainly not with the precise insight I possess." Her tone grew more seductive. "I'm the source you seek, Michael Mansford. Through my eyes, you shall see."

By gosh, she spoke Surrogate's words, and if so, then there was no doubt she was the key to unlocking this confounding mystery.

The mask beamed brighter, catching his eye, its twinkling hue turning silver, then gold, then bronze, before settling on a smooth, copper gleam, which in turn rippled, sloshing forth to create a million, microscopic, cranking gears, which in his convoluted mind, soon became an enormous, clicking sphere.

He envisioned the little, green men, with Sontar leading the charge, the hulking shadows stretching longer, engulfing them, their point of origin yet ineffable, but insinuating the chance to grow more defined...

In an instant, the scene dissolved, and the mask readapted its pearly sheen.

Mansford was at a loss for words, and his silence spurred Montorto to say: "What you envisioned stems from what you absorbed in the field, or more precisely what the Persona deciphered through your combined mind's eye, but I—and only I—can show the full extent of what is coming. I have a unique inclination, as you've well admitted, and when abetted by your mystical abilities, such will clarify any situation, including the one that's about to spread. We can do this, Michael Mansford—together, but if we hesitate...."

Mansford felt compelled to consent. After all, it was more than the woman's sensual tone that influenced him. She knew something, and by all means, he had to know what it was.

"Are you there?" she asked.

His eyes fell upon the side table, where Standish's framed portrait stood, reminding him of how she had once led him to stumble. It had given the Great Beguiler leverage. What if something similar now occurred? Of course, he would never betray his lady fair, but still, there was no denying Montorto's ability to enchant. Was his mortal side—his fallible side—strong enough to withstand the lure?

"Please, answer me," Montorto continued. "I know you're listening."

"Yes, I'm here." He rubbed his eyes and refocused, his pretentiousness wavering. "So you want to meet. That's fine, but I warn you, if the slightest thing feels off balance, I'll sever ties right then and there. Understood, Miss Montorto?"

A long pause followed, capped by a sheepish purr. "Yes…yes, of course, I understand."

"Very well. Now, where are we to cross paths?"

"The Top Hat Dining Court," she said without hesitation.

"Top Hat? I'd hardly call it conducive to conversation, let alone privacy. It's perpetually packed. I doubt we'll be able to think, let alone—"

"It'll be fine," she assured him, "safe for me, safe for you. I'll reserve us a nice niche, well beyond the hustle-and-bustle."

"And the time?"

"Tomorrow evening—seven," she said. "Does that suit you?"

"Yes," Mansford agreed. "Seven works."

"I'll look forward to seeing you, Mister Mansford." She sighed deeply. "Have a lovely evening."

He stared at the receiver, realizing he could only hope for the best now. One thing was certain: if things did go awry, he would give his saintly mentor a hardy piece of his mind. On the other hand, another option yet lingered. Who said he should go alone? Certainly, it would be unwise to take Standish, but there was another whose presence might work to his advantage.

With a contented grin, he clicked the phone and dialed Father Bruno.

IV

A tall, top-hatted gent, who looked much like the cartoonish neon sign atop the building's facade, spotted Mansford nearing. He tipped his brim and opened the door.

"Good evening, Mister Mansford. Nice to see you again, sir. Enjoy your visit."

Mansford slipped him a ten and entered. Soft trumpet music greeted him as he headed toward the gaunt, balding, mustached maitre d' stationed behind the reservations stand.

The man smiled. "Good evening, Mister Mansford." He looked down at his ledger and struck the entrepreneur's name from the log with his pen. He then looked about and clicked his fingers, signaling a spiffy, fair-haired youth with cloth-draped arm to approach.

"Please seat Mister Mansford per the requested specifications," the maitre d' instructed, which dropped the youth into a respectful bow. With a subtle turn of his heels, the lad then lead Mansford toward the main dining room.

Mansford scanned the surroundings: the high, dark walls, the many centered tables, the dim, side booths where shady characters smoked and amorous couples cuddled. In the distance, a red-lit stage beckoned, a sharp-dressed trumpeter continuing to toot his smooth, non-descript tune, his matching band mates banging, strumming… swaying.

The young man looked back to ensure Mansford was in tow and gestured him past an unassuming booth, where a cherubic-faced, bearded man sat, his crisp, white collar visible in the hazy glow, a bottle of wine and a bowl of spaghetti before him.

Father Bruno and Mansford exchanged inconspicuous glances. Mansford had, in fact, asked Stark to phone the club that day, ensuring the priest would be stationed in the area where he and Montorto were to sit, but much to Mansford's dismay, the young man marched onward.

Mansford slowed, cleared his throat, tempted to ask the youngster if he had missed his mark, but then he spotted Montorto's crossed, stilettoed legs protruding beneath the far-end table, a decent distance away.

"Here you are, sir," said the lad as he approached he table, giving another bow and a dramatic wave, "just as the lady requested. Oh, silly me, allow me to take your—"

"No thank you," Mansford answered, tugging the collar around his neck. "I'm fine." He reached into his pocket. "Here you go, son. Appreciate the service."

"Uh, no need, sir," the youngster croaked. "All's covered, including the meal, drinks and entertainment: house rules, at least for our more prestigious guests."

Mansford smiled and glanced back at Father Bruno, who squirmed a tad.

Mansford threw the priest a subtle shrug, thanked the young man and without a peep of protest entered the booth, squeezing next to the perfumed Montorto, acknowledging her with a slight nod, while his eyes absorbed her demeanor: pink, dark-lensed glasses and a sheer blouse, beneath which her black bra seeped.

She smirked and in a near whisper, sang in perfect synch to the band's new tune:

" 'When the deep purple falls over the sleepy wall…and the stars begin to twinkle in the sky…in the midst of a memory you'll come back to me… breathing my name with a sigh…' "

Mansford cracked a smile, finding the moment silly, if not embarrassing.

She sensed his chagrin and raised her spectacles.

"Hello, Mister Mansford," she cooed, her pupils sparkling. "It's so nice to see you." She twirled her finger at the stage. "Don't you just love 'Deep Purple'? Such a stirring melody: perfect for setting the mood."

"Yeah," Mansford concurred. "Catchy."

The young man returned and asked, "Would either of you like a drink?" He pointed to Montorto's empty glass. "More brandy, perhaps?"

"No," she said, pushing her spectacles upward and shaking her head, "I'm fine for now. Besides, three's generally my limit." She snickered and turned to Mansford. "What about you, dear?"

"Water." He tried to look amiable but professional. "Maybe toss in some ice while you're at it. All right, son?"

"Yes, Mister Mansford," the youth consented. "Be back in a jiffy."

Mansford returned his attention to his comely consort. "Just as I expected, the place is jammed, and this on-the-house deal, it's a first for me. Your doing, Miss Montorto?"

She did not respond, appearing lost in her thoughts, continuing to purr, " '…And as long as my heart will beat, we'll always meet, here in my purple dreams…' "

As lovely as she was, Mansford's patience began to wane. Source or no source, he would not be played the fool. "Maybe this wasn't such a good idea, Miss Montorto." He started to squeeze out of the booth. "Thanks for the indulgence—"

She sprung up and as she had done before upon his threatened exit, grabbed his arm. Her grip was tight, stronger than he would have suspected.

"Don't go," she begged. "Please, I was trying to get into the right mode to ensure an effective rapport." She loosened her grip and tossed off her glasses, mesmerizing him with her beckoning stare. She then slithered her svelte frame against his side and leaning forth, placed her lips to his ear. "Come now. Have a little faith."

This prompted him to glance at Father Bruno. He swallowed hard, stunned as the priest began to march toward them, the imprint of Standish projecting from out his urgent scowl.

As Father Bruno neared, Mansford craned his neck, feigned a surprised grin. "Oh, yes, uh, Father Bruno—what a surprise. What brings you here, padre?"

"Figured I'd get a bite," the father growled, but then realized he had overstepped his bounds. "Spotted you on your way in and didn't wish to leave without saying hello...or good-bye, as the case may be."

It was then that two strong-jawed men with puffy cheeks and cauliflower ears, bolted from a side booth. In an instant, they were upon the priest and grabbed him from behind.

"Hey, what's the big idea?" Mansford exclaimed, springing out of the booth. "Let go of him, I say. He's a friend of mine—a priest, for God's sake. Show some respect." The men looked at Mansford, but only tightened their grip, making Father Bruno wince. Mansford felt his skin tingle, felt the urge to conjure his alter-ego, but managed to restrain the sensation. "I said let him go. He only came over to chat."

"His kind ain't allowed here," the taller of the thugs answered, pinching the father's collar. "Too bad we missed the obvious. We've rules, you know, for when we hold parties here. This here's um...uh, a sec-err...a secular gathering."

"No," said the shorter one with a nudge. "You got it wrong. You and I are secular. These other folks are, uh, different in their views. Remember?"

"Oh, yeah," the big goof uttered, still glaring at the priest. "These folks here are different—different than you, you see."

"There you go," said the shorter. "That means we don't want any judgmental jerks spoilin' the atmosphere for this payin' party. Get the drift?"

"Oh, please," Father Bruno groaned, and with one mighty thrust, broke from the thugs. "What gives you the right to say who stays or goes? Need I remind you, this is still the United States of America?"

"Watch your step, holy man," the taller one warned, raising his fist. "We've every right to—"

Mansford forced himself between the thugs, his heels hinting to rise, when from around the bend, a man dressed in a sharp, tan suit, sporting a monocle and bushy mustache, neared. With a slight German accent, he commanded, "Hank—that's enough." He turned to the shorter. "That goes for you, too, Josh. Let the poor priest be. It's obvious he's Mister Mansford's acquaintance." He smiled and adjusted his monocle.

Mansford regarded the man with caution. "And you are, sir?"

"I'm the young lady's confidant," he replied, avoiding Mansford's gaze to scan Montorto's leggy frame, "Herr Hans Gut, but most refer to me as Mister Good."

"I see," Mansford said. "Confidant, you say?"

Good avoided the question. "Hank...Josh...that will be all."

The men exchanged confused looks before shuffling away, back to their booth.

Others continued to regard the proceedings, but when Good turned to them, they glanced down, resuming their meals and conversation, absorbing the breezy music that continued as if nothing had happened.

Good looked at Mansford and this time answered, his pitch more affirmative. "Yes, confidant: an interesting way to describe our relationship, but please don't misconstrue the meaning. If anything, Mister Mansford, I am arguably at best the lady's quasi-mentor."

Mansford glared at Good and then signaled Father Bruno to his side. "You okay?" he whispered.

"Sure, Michael. So sorry I jumped the gun." The priest blushed. "I got a tad nervous on Miss Standish's part, I dare say, when I saw you and the lady, well…"

"I sincerely apologize for the misunderstanding," Good interrupted, raising his voice a notch higher, "but Miss Montorto is a most specialized, team member, for a lack of a better term: one of infinite mental capacity, and for the sake of our recent alliance, I did insist upon the enforcement of her welfare, which is why my men came forth. They are trained, you see, to act quickly."

"Indeed," Mansford commented with distaste.

Montorto sighed. "It's just the way we handle things," she explained, with sweet enunciation. "It applies to anyone of an opposing, theological viewpoint. The father is of that ilk. Anyway, I can generally sense a bad aura coming from a mile away, but I'm not always quick enough to deflect it, particularly if I'm distracted by an attractive man." She fluttered her lashes. "Hans and the boys can attest to that."

Mansford grimaced. "Interesting. I'd have assumed that you'd deduce that Father Bruno and I embrace the same beliefs." He then shot Good a sly squint. "With that confirmed, I wonder if I'm still permitted in your fold."

Good chuckled. "Of course, Mister Mansford. Your spiritual strengths work on multiple levels, or rather, your alter-ego's. You may consider yourself Christian, but you are, from a philosophical and metaphysical vantage, so much more."

Father Bruno tugged Manford's arm. "I fear we have a loon on our hands, Michael." The priest sneered at Good. "Cut the crazy talk, mister. It's not making you look very credible."

Again, Good chuckled. "See my point, Mister Mansford? You only let your subjects share pieces of your grand plans, and only when such suits you. That speaks volumes." Good then raised a dismissive hand to Father Bruno. "Pardon my bluntness, padre, but you're out of your league here. Witch doctors—civilized or not—simply have no place in our specialized sect."

The statement stunned Mansford, and he cupped the priest's shoulders in support. "I've heard enough silly pomp and circumstance for one night," he said and with a gentle shove, guided his friend away.

"Uh, please, Mister Mansford," Good stammered, stepping toward them. "I do apologize. The words—they came out wrong." He wrung his hands with pretentious fervor. "I am, alas, an unabashed snob when it comes to the spiritual medium. Truly, I find Catholicism no less dignified than any other Christian creed." He gave Father Bruno a humble nod. "It's just my, uh, unique form of expression. Again, truly, I'm sorry."

Father Bruno frowned and continued on with his friend, who kept a firm grip on his arm, but then Montorto reached out and grabbed Mansford's coat, yanking him (and the priest) backward.

She pressed behind Mansford, directing her whispery breath upon his neck. "I implore you, don't go. Why should a minor misstep ruin our plans?" She paused, her breath beating harder. "You do want to know about the little people, don't you?"

Mansford did, of course, but not under such stifling circumstances. He would just have to get the information through some other means (and perhaps through some better direction from the saint). With a stiff jerk, he shook Montorto loose and again headed with the father toward the door.

The music slowed, with the trumpeter punctuating the matter with a dissonant blurt. This ushered the band into a noisy abstraction, whereupon the crimson lights below the stage flickered in demented synch, leading Mansford to wonder if such may have been planned as a back-up distraction.

In any event, the cacophony made Mansford's body reverberate. "Now, what's this?" he asked, turning to Montorto. "I say, what's going on?"

Good skidded forth. "No need to panic, Mister Mansford." He looked to those seated, particularly those who dared look his way. "It's just the way we express ourselves, under moments of...well, potential duress. A celebratory spurt is always good for the soul."

The music then stopped; the lights steadied, and those who had glanced at Good rose from out their booths, their movements sluggish, strange, as were their projected shadows, which in their elongated extensions implied a life of their own, wavering within some sort of weird, collective haze.

Father Bruno whispered, "I don't know what's going on, Michael, but whatever it is, I've a real bad feeling about it. Any suggestions?"

Though Mansford did not reply, the priest felt a change in his friend's solidity, which in turn seeped into the cleric's arm, allowing the priest to remember Ben Gyler and the Persona's crusade against him. Perhaps, Father

Bruno thought, such a conflict had come again.

"Stay within my proximity," Mansford instructed and began to ascend. "I'll scope the vicinity for a way out. If need be, reach up, and I'll elevate you."

"Sure, sure, Michael," Father Bruno stammered, "whatever you say, son. Whatever you say."

Mansford's outer coat fell to the floor. The priest looked up and saw the sweep of a scarf, the deadly gleam of a dagger and upon his friend's face, the magnetic mask.

Montorto noticed the transformation, too, and without further ado, scoped the surroundings, trying to ascertain how many more of Good's ensemble approached.

The Persona's majestic aura rained down, flowing outward, further saturating Father Bruno's mind, allowing his senses to expand from a number of kaleidoscopic angles, absorbing sporadic, dark thoughts and designs: goose-stepping soldiers, raising their arms in contemptuous salutes...deafening cheers engulfing militant parades and speeches...misguided hearts that harbored resentment toward those adverse to their mad cause...

Though such sensations were misguided, Father Bruno also realized their genesis stemmed only from people, not monsters, not Guaners, not anything like what the Great Beguiler would conjure. What spewed forth here could be severed, stepped on... dispatched.

The Persona swung his dagger in lofty, symbolic jest, his mind swatting the shuffling fools to the floor. He encircled the band, toppling its members from off the stage, while Montorto trailed his every move, skipping in unison with him, her eyes peeled and piercing until they met the priest's, and then turned icy.

Father Bruno sensed her contempt, her jealousy, her desire to be the Persona's consort, and into the cleric's mind, she rammed all of her contempt. In an instant, the holy man's consciousness slipped, and he slumped downward.

The Persona descended, his gaze fixed on Montorto, his countenance mirroring a myriad of tones: old, young, male, female, most demented, disgruntled and mean. They represented her, and she knew it.

The Persona slid alongside the priest and knelt, shaking the gossamer projections of his assailants away, back into their fleshy shells, making many stumble into one another with comical panache.

He sensed Good's steely stare upon him, while maintaining Montorto's desperate vibes. He wished to strike them both down and would have, if not for Father Bruno's enveloping pain.

The Persona stretched his gloved fingers across the unconscious man's brow,

"Stay within my proximity..."

but then felt something hard whack the back of his head.

The Persona's mortal part—that gnawing, anchoring human element within—throbbed and bled. Michael Mansford rose from out, eclipsing the Persona's celestial flow, the mask growing cold and stiff against his face. He cranked his arm upward, attempting to hoist the dagger, but in vain.

His eyes rolled upward, absorbing a dripping bottle of wine in Good's white-knuckled hand. He heard Montorto gasp, and then he looked to Father Bruno, his eyes fluttering as their intertwined consciousness faded, the creaky recollection of "Deep Purple" inundating in their brains.

V

Manford woke within a heavy haze, the gentle pre-summer breeze coddling his pounding brow, the outer glare bright and violet. He knew he failed. It was now a matter of how much so.

He still wore the mask, his coat, scarf…gloves, the dagger placed at his side.

Good clicked his heels. "Guten morgen, Herr Mansford," he declared. "Do you hear me, Mister Persona? Are you cognitive, sir?"

Mansford mustered a hoarse, "Go to hell," and the snide German laughed.

Mansford heard Father Bruno groan nearby and breathed the warm grass. "Where are we?" he asked.

"In a field," said Good, "a very lovely one, at that. In fact, from what Miss Montorto has informed me, one you've already visited."

The thought of the little, green creatures racked Mansford's mind. He should not have been so flippant about their presence, let alone anyone connected to them. How could he have been so naïve; how could the Persona…?

"So," grumbled Mansford, forcing his focus, "this was your intent all along, a way to trick me, get me back here, but why didn't you just stake me out, bludgeon me the first time around?" His head throbbed from the excruciating illogic of it. "What was the point?"

Good emerged like a ghost from a fog and knelt, the sun surrounding his head like an evil halo. For a moment, he seemed to study Mansford, evidently sizing him up.

Mansford cranked upward and managed to sit. He lifted his mask, fixing it above his brow like the brim of a hat. A cool breeze stroked his cheeks: more mocking than comforting.

"Yes, yes," said Good with relish, "I see the awareness in your eyes…and the fear. There's no need for you to outguess. We will take care of everything from here. The odds did not favor such an outcome, but you let your distrust mount, and well... To be honest, we actually anticipated the worse when reservations were made for one named Bruno Ugliano... an orphan priest, no less, or so we came to discover. We felt no need to interfere necessarily, but hoped your friend might at least relegate himself to the backdrop and enjoy the atmosphere." Good clucked his tongue. "Pity it turned out otherwise."

Mansford followed Good's gaze toward Father Bruno, who was sandwiched between the nightclub henchmen, his wrists bound, his body twisted and for better or worse, cognitive.

A short distance behind him Montorto stood, the wind ruffling her dress, revealing her lovely legs. She avoided Mansford's gaze, but he knew she was aware of his stare.

"Perhaps," she commented, "matters would have gone as planned if I had only been given the allotted time, perhaps even a more secluded sector. The idea was to charm him, after all, make him subscribe to our cause, not turn things adversarial at the drop of a hat."

"Everyone was there," said Good, "everyone, that is, who could have influenced the Persona's position, but the feel was wrong, because he was wrong, and above all, I now suspect that thanks to you, my dear, we've wasted yet another moment, another precious day to invest in our mission."

Nervous murmurs rose, and Mansford realized more people had entered the scene. Based on their bleary-eyed demeanor, he knew they were from the nightclub, and even recognized a few of their soured faces.

As the seconds slipped by, the sky lightened, allowing Mansford to absorb more of the locale, which was, indeed, the little men's realm, but where, oh, where were they?

He gazed into the higher patches of grass, around the trees, through the bushes, but saw no insinuating shapes, no movement, except for where the breeze skimmed.

"Be assured, Mister Mansford," said Good, "the entities are here. They merely need an abrupt atmospheric push or shove to become visible. Their manifestation is multi-layered, to say the least, unless one like the Persona were to assist, but evidently he's dormant." Good sneered. "Isn't that right, sir?"

The remark enraged Mansford, for he knew Good was right. He only wished he could ignite his inner fervor, but try as he may, it remained stagnant.

"The Persona will come forth," Mansford declared, cloaking his uncertainty, "when he sees fit." He threw back his shoulders, tried to look tough, even though the mask slid a notch down his brow. "Until then, you'll just have to deal with me, and I assure you, you're likely to find me as tenacious as my alter-ego."

"Oh, my," said Good with a pretentious shiver. "I certainly won't take your threat in stride. The most startling deeds often stem from mere mortals, or so my homeland has demonstrated on more than several occasions. Anything supernatural is only icing on the cake, but in your case, well...." He shook his head, bit his lip. "Nonetheless, perhaps you might yet muster enough to surprise."

"Don't trust him," Father Bruno warned, but the henchmen silenced him each with a swift kick.

"It's all right," cried Mansford, hoping his compliance would subdue them. He then forced himself up and looked Good straight in the eye. "What do you have in mind?"

Before Good could answer, there came a great swoosh, a reverberating thud, a whizzing that whirled several times over, causing those gathered to wobble and fall.

"What the—" Mansford exclaimed.

A strange, purple mist invaded the air, peppered by random, flashing spurts which cascaded at various points around the perimeter.

After a moment, folks grabbed onto one another for support, seeming to accept the phenomenon with a curious ease.

Mansford watched the trumpeter waddle among them and commence a few, dry notes of "Deep Purple," before one of his band mates skidded forth and nudged him into restraint.

Despite the strangeness, Good appeared most pleased, especially when Montorto backed into him. He wrapped his arms around her and chuckled, "See my dear—see it never fails. It's like magic—pure, uninhibited magic each and every time."

"Yes...yes...I see," she gasped. "It's like the greatest sorcery ever conceived." She slipped from Good's grasp and waved her fingers in the air. "Oh, my— they're coming, Hans. See? They're coming."

Mansford braced his mask, if only to keep it sliding onto his face, and in the process, his vision cleared. He heard—or was it more, imagined?— applause, some, laughter. He sensed some prancing, people pointing about, as little, green limbs protruded from out what might be the sheerest of veils, manifesting near and far, throughout various grassy clumps.

Mansford saw Sontar's gnomish cranium rise, haloed by a silvery haze which beamed off his metal crown as he squeezed from out of long, dimensional slits, like a baby popping from a womb, and stumbled, with his splotchy robe yet in development, across the billowing blades.

His beady eyes met Mansford's, instilling within the man an unexpected spark of both apprehension and glee.

Sontar's expression grew grim, and without missing a beat, he beseeched, "Help us, Persona. Help us, please." He flapped his elongating cape with his arms, forcing a sword to extend from his palm. "You must help us. You must."

Mansford swallowed his suspicions and opened his mind. *"Must what?"* he asked, or was it the Persona? *"What...what exactly must I do?"*

Sontar looked behind him. "Fight," he squeaked, his voice tense and rushed. "You must help us fight the enemy."

An enormous, animalistic roar rose in the distance, followed by a belligerent, reverberating bugle. This prompted the quivering trumpeter to answer it with an equally long blurt: by no means as indignant, but penetrating all the same.

With a click of his heels, Good leapt back, as did most of the others, gathering along the sides, leaving only Manford and Montorto among the tiny, scurrying army.

Montorto regarded Mansford with grave concern. "Sontar is right," she said. "We must fight these monsters, ward them off...if need be, kill them. This is why we wanted you here...to see if you could fulfill the task, and if not—well, if not, we'd have no choice but to shut the experiment down, or find some other elusive locale to reengage it." Her breasts heaved in anticipation. "I begged Hans to give you another chance by tossing you straight into the lion's den." She grinned, but her anxiousness still shined through. "I know you can do it. I told Hans, you could. Don't prove me wrong."

Under the circumstances, how could Mansford deny her? The moment's urgency allowed no pause, and yet, in glancing at the still constrained Father Bruno, he felt compelled to say, "Release him. Release him now and I'll help—help in any way I can."

Good turned to his thugs and snapped his fingers.

They obeyed, and Mansford sensed Father Bruno's relief as they cut him loose. The Persona's dominance then mounted, his aura twinkling, tingling, rising in intensity, as he rose off the ground and the mask slipped down.

"It's working...working," Mansford's mind echoed, crawling back into his subconscious. *"I can see...see them coming."*

Another roar erupted; along with another horn.

"If you're going to do something," Good said, stretching upon his toes, watching the Persona ascend, "you had better do it now. The beasts are at the hilltop."

Like the snap of a trap, the Persona's expanding consciousness clamped down upon their location and ensuing descent, watching the creatures crackle from out a roll of purple mist.

They were broad shouldered and thick-necked, in some ways resembling the Guaners, towering above human height, but upon keener inspection, it was clear they were bipedal and garbed in chainmail, ragged furs, horns extending from the sides of their knobby, steel caps, their arms muscular, their faces jowly, their noses upturned, and like their smaller counterparts, green-skinned.

"Get the little ones," the burliest brute blabbered in English so garbled the Persona had trouble discerning it. "Cut them down." The oaf lumbered fast from the center cluster, as another to his left blew a hateful, brass horn. "Make the wee bastards bleed."

With guttural hoots and hollers, the blubbery giants stomped downward, their booted feet thundering upon the earth, their gleaming blades swiping the air.

Like an avenging angle, the Persona swooped toward them, his scarf slapping about like a riled rattler, his gleaming dagger aimed from his gloved hand, his face a simmering ray that spread like a long, white spear across the attackers' collective scowls. He absorbed their features, and in so doing, probed deep and hard into their pasts, only to find they possessed none. It was as though they were propelled only by preprogrammed motivation.

The creatures slowed under the weight of his presence, their piercing, black orbs angling up at his haunting, hovering shape.

"Aaarrrggghhh," their leader cried, as the others merged around him, raising their weapons before their faces, as to shield themselves from an inevitable strike.

"Oh, the glare is strong," the leader whimpered, tears streaming down his droopy cheeks. "Mercy, mercy, dear angelic specter—please, please, please dim your light."

Though compassionate, the Persona was not foolish, intending to release the beasts only if they retreated to wherever they had sprung; but there was another force intermingling with his own. He homed in on it and gazed down upon Montorto, whose stilettos were anchored in the ground, her arms outstretched, her fingers fanned.

Sontar and his soldiers danced about her, several pointing and laughing at their opponent's sobs, which grew muffled under the woman's bristling energy: a steady, drowning sound, like wind trapped within a tunnel, crashing in upon itself.

"*Stand down and go back,*" her mind cried to the cowering behemoths, "*or face the consequences.*"

Though under other circumstances, the Persona may have appreciated her efforts, he did not desire her help at the moment, nor did he relish her brashness. In scorn, he harnessed the flow of her mental prowess, tapping such from her spirit and funneling it into his own and from there, hammered it down upon the marauders.

The brutes blasted backward, stumbling into one another much as had the night-club participants, but the creatures seemed far more frightened and confused. In panic, they snorted and squealed, clawing and stumbling over one another to reach the hill.

Good leapt and clapped. "Ah, look at them go, like scared, little piggies." He then laughed to the point of choking. "Bravo! Magnifico! A splendid display, Mister Persona. A most splendid display, indeed."

Exhausted, Montorto fell to her knees. Beyond her evident fatigue, the Persona knew she would endure, and as such kept his mind's eye on the brutes' trail, watching them reach the hilltop, clawing through what he now discerned as a larger veil, which spewed random, purple plumes upon them grazing their brawny frames.

Good, still guffawing, skipped toward Montorto, with little concern for the leaping, little creatures he nearly stomped and offered her his hand. She responded with a spiteful turn of her head, though her disdain was, in truth, aimed more at the Persona.

The Persona continued watching the behemoths depart, letting his mind scope the vicinity for any possible stragglers, or any additional, odd activity, and (as was no surprise) detected such along the fringes, where behind several large, trees, dark-coated, scholarly scowling men tinkered behind at large, cylindrical contraptions, propped by wide, triangular bases. Why had he not detected them sooner?

The objects beamed a hypnotic, chrome sheen, which appeared to absorb the sun's rays, turning such back into apparent balls of swirling, purple dust. The coated men adjusted their spectacles, inspecting the fronts and backs of each device, of which there were four, two along each side, with about fifty feet between them. The men were far too immersed in the objects to acknowledge the Persona's approach, and on this basis, the specter realized, they were unaware he had expelled the beasts.

The Persona slid toward the object nearest the densest gathering of men, around which a group of the gleeful, tiny folks jumped and hoorayed.

Good had by this time abandoned Montorto, having followed the Persona to the mechanism and smiled at its hypnotic hum.

"Most intriguing," said the Persona. The coated men finally looked at him, dumbstruck. He waved his dagger at the contraption, his face gleaming of suspicion and turned to Good. "Would you tell me, Herr Gut, what these contraptions are, or would you prefer I simply snatch such from your mind?"

Good's face grew stony. "They are dimensional churners. They pulsate in such a way to open portals." He smiled, in hopes that such might change the subject. "I must say, I have renewed my faith in you—and again in Miss Montorto—but I sense you have doubts about me. No matter. You did precisely what she predicted, and next time—"

"I've no desire for a next time," the Persona stated, "and the current circumstances seem likely to worsen, unless you level with me."

"Do what he says," Montorto huffed, culling enough strength to stand. "His powers are far superior to anything any of us can conjure. I suppose if he wanted, he could crush our minds, Hans. Why anger him?"

"All right," Good grumbled, "I'll level with him if you wish."

Montorto nodded at the Persona, and he at her, prompting Good to turn and with another punctuating click, he commenced: "Our group has been looking into inter-dimensional rifts for some time, though we had no idea what we might find. Surely, you must realize, sir, we are dealing with...or rather have awakened...a most extreme, adversarial force, and considering the endangerment of these poor, little specimens, we constructed machinery to assist their cause. The sooner the enemy would be allowed to come through, the sooner we could dispatch them...at least if we had the right weapon, or more precisely, the right individual."

The Persona shook his head at the foolishness of it all. "These mechanisms," he countered, "are the reason these creatures have manifested." He regarded the coated men, who squirmed, studying him from behind their thick lenses. "In that regard, I do not believe they are the products of another dimension. You've made them somehow, imprinted them with specific physical and behavioral designs." He glanced at Sontar, who had crept up from the side, his stance defensive, suspicious. "How else would they know English—and accent-free, I might add—even smoother than that of Herr Gut?"

"We simply listen," Sontar interjected, as his men ended their revelry and regarded their leader with curious concern. "We learn."

"Ah, I see," the Persona said, returning the dagger to his hip. "How admirable. You listen and adapt the native tongue, though I thought you attained the language by reading Miss Montorto's mind. In any event, your aggressors have obviously adapted the same approach. Yes, most admirable, indeed." The mask softened and smirked. "Tell me, how much of the human world do you know, and how did you come to choose entrance into it at this time. Is it truly just a coincidence?"

Father Bruno made his way over. "You're onto something, Michael," he whispered. "I sense it. There's something insincere about these little ones… something, I dare say, unholy."

"The only thing you sense," said Sontar, "is your overactive imagination." He placed a hand upon his hip, twirled his sword and then skipped past the priest, so he could focus solely on the specter. "How we came to be, how we came to know the things we know, is of little consequence. It matters only that we exist—exist now only a few steps beyond your backyard—and despite what you say, we have been in grave need of help, which you have graciously granted." He sighed. "Surely, you'd not have helped us if you sensed we were in any way deceitful, if not evil."

The king made a valid point, but the Persona was hesitant to embrace it. He still wished to read what dwelled inside the creature's head, but as with the larger beasts, failed to discern any clear intent and disgruntled, he turned again to Good.

"Don't look at me that way," Good blurted. "I don't have the answers. Whatever the wee king can offer is the best you'll likely to get."

The Persona said nothing, just fixed on Good's gaze, bouncing between naked eye and monocled one, breaking through a series of long nurtured, intensive barriers, until he found a rush of thoughts and ideas.

The Persona saw stiff, marching soldiers, Roman-esque columns, between which uniformed men stood at podiums, Herr Gut in their midst. Good listened to them with manic fervor, shaking hands, assuring those he met that he was their man…moving on behind closed doors, among the coated men now gathered, milling through steel shards and heavy metal, making the pieces fit, click, sputter and spew, purple smoke seeping from their unsoldered seams.

"Aaahhh," Good screamed, as if burnt. He cupped his face and tripped backward, peering between his fingers as he growled, "You ghastly, self-righteous thing—how dare you invade my thoughts."

The Persona offered no apology, just turned, letting Good's frightened features fade from his own. He then turned to Sontar and with pity, looked upon the creature.

"You are, indeed, fabricated," he said, "programmed to live, talk and play within this strange game, whatever its intent." He looked to the hilltop. "The same goes for your aggressors: more actors upon the grassy stage."

"No, Persona," Sontar spouted, "you're wrong, and regardless of our cause, we truly have every reason to fear. Perhaps, we always will. Those behemoths will slaughter us for certain." He threw down his blade, stepped forward, placing his fingers above and below his eyes, making them bulge. "If you don't believe me, take a look. See for yourself. I've nothing to hide."

With a stoic turn, the Persona declined; aware he would find nothing but preprogrammed impressions in the specimen's mind.

"This is an experiment gone wrong," the Persona continued, his tone soft and contemplative, then walked—or was it glided?—toward Montorto. "You invited me to this field, assuming you would participate in what become a historic, paranormal event, but I wonder, why make the phenomenon manifest at all, let alone in this locale? Why should these people come all this way to conduct what could have just as well transpired in Germany?"

Montorto trembled and seethed, "Because those of the SIIS don't subscribe to the Nazi philosophy, any more than any other traditions of faith. Contrary to what you presume, SIIS members are extremely insightful and ethical. If you'd only toss your prejudices away and do your job, perhaps then you'd see."

"Herr Gut's thoughts contradict your claim," the Persona replied. "He's broken bread with bad men, and from what I can deduct, with impunity."

"I did what was necessary," said Good, "so I might know what was happening behind the scenes. Miss Montorto is right. You've only scratched the surface, Persona. You must toss your prejudices aside, open your mind."

"I have," said the Persona with somber conviction. "I've had far more than enough, and there's nothing more repellent to me than those who dare play god." He turned to Father Bruno. I'm wondering if you should return to Miss Montorto's home. You could call the precinct; ask for Jack Murphy, perhaps. I'm sure he wouldn't mind investigating the matter. Perhaps he might even send some squad cars to round up those responsible for the danger this situation poses." He looked down at Sontar, and formed a long frown. "Alas, as for these poor creatures, a fair sum of scrutiny must be applied."

"We will not be scrutinized," the little king decried, "poked or prodded by your scholarly charlatans. We'd rather fend for ourselves...die, if need be."

"You needn't worry," Good said, waving his finger at the perimeter. "The dimensional passage is loosening—should be gone in less than an hour. You'll be in your niche, and we in ours, even if in unwarranted custody, but when the next time comes, I assure you, it'll be without opposition." He turned to the Persona. "But, you already know this, don't you, sir?" He laughed. "Yes... so much for hollow threats."

The Persona paused, then nodded, more out of polite necessity than sincerity.

Sontar's face contorted with doubt, as Good and the others walked away, leaving only the Persona and Montorto to linger, but when Sontar turned his back to them, his subjects followed suit, leaving the two mystics no other recourse than to depart.

"I fear for them," Montorto said. "They need more than a reprieve. Those beasts will, indeed, try again, and there's no way they can ward them off, considering their great size and strength."

"They're fortunate we entered the scene when we did," said the Persona, his gait meshing with Mansford's, "but when the situation is staged...well, what does it matter now, with the variables in motion?"

The Persona felt his exterior fade, along with the confines of the niche, so that by the time the two passed the brush, Mansford had resumed normal form, and the little people, for all intents and purposes, had become an intangible memory.

"To think," said Montorto with flippant grace, "that they live and breathe despite what logic dictates. It's amazing...miraculous, regardless of your theory."

Mansford regarded the wavering grass, the swaying branches, the now dormant devices, cooling toward dying hums, knowing far too well that the strangest things did, in fact, reside beyond one's immediate grasp. However, with these creatures, the cause was different. They did not emanate from any aged, celestial scope. They were part of the here-and-now, confined somehow within it. Why, oh why, had the Persona not yet targeted their genesis, the reason they came to be?

"Escort your guests back to your house," Mansford instructed her. "Engage in whatever niceties you see fit. I'll take it from there."

She appeared confused, perhaps even offended by his brashness, but then sighed and scampered onward, cutting past the band members to catch up with Good and whisper in his ear.

Good slowed, looked back, then to his entourage blared, "We're going to spend some time at Miss Montorto's abode. She has tea and cookies for us. It will give us time to relax, to garner our thoughts, so that we may better ruminate on this morning's events."

He shot Mansford a curt glance that seemed to ask, "Did that suffice?"

Mansford answered with a knowing smirk and continued across the field, his gaze falling upon the many cars parked alongside the gloomy home.

VI

"**T**he machines are not what you presume," said Good, pacing before his audience in the dim living room. "They clear the so-called veil via vibrations. They do not in any way fabricate life, Mister Mansford. Surely if that were the case, your insightful alter-ego would have detected it, but I sense hesitation on the Persona's part. At best, he has no better a handle on this than you."

Mansford watched Good swagger about, his fanfare eyeing him with assurance nibbling their cookies, sipping their cinnamon tea. They appeared anything but troubled, like fixtures in their own right: organic decorations in a play.

"Perhaps," said Mansford, maintaining his calm. "In any event, you claim you've experienced similar phenomena in your homeland, and to replicate such, these remarkable mechanisms were constructed. That's all well and fine, but again I ask, why not experiment in your own back yard. Why go to America, to little ol' Brink Town, to test your hand? I don't buy the Nazi angle. You could hide from them, I'm sure." He then glanced at Montorto, who was leaning against the far wall alongside the tight-jawed Father Bruno and the adjacent henchmen, her eyes wide and gleaming. "You were the one who discovered, or at least acknowledged, the vibrations, Miss Montorto, and the specimens they spewed forth. You reached out to your colleagues as a result. Correct?"

"All SIIS members subscribe to the same agenda," Montorto said. "It's the SIIS way, if you will. We stay in contact, always sharing ideas, so we might better understand the paranormal."

"Miss Montorto," Good interjected, moving toward her, "has kept us abreast of the atmospheric shifts in this area, and all well before the creatures made their appearance. We became most curious and so made our sojourn."

Mansford raised an eyebrow. "Atmospheric shifts, eh?" He pushed between her and Good and as before, reached out and brushed back Montorto's hair, but this time did not tug. "Would you care to elaborate?"

Montorto shrugged. "They're shifts within the air, from what I can ascertain, from out which dreams sometimes come…disturbing dreams, that is, that locals have cautiously substantiated in their various conversations about town." She batted her lashes. "Surely, Mister Mansford, you know of such." She paused, then stated, "I presume the lovely Miss Standish has even shared a few such references during the course of your relationship."

Indeed, Standish had admitted to strange reveries and even on occasion detailed the hideous Guaners, as well as Ben Gyler, the Great Beguiler, who had warped her mind and turned her into a political puppet.

But dreams were dreams. To keep sweet Standish at ease, he had told her that her parents perished in an unsavory, artifact-smuggling mishap, and the less she recalled of what had truly happened, the better. As for the manifestation of monsters, well, they were just a result of the ambiguous pain; and for better or worse, such lies were warranted when the truth might prove too maddening.

"Well, did she ever mention such?" Montorto restated.

"On occasion," Mansford confessed, "but really, that's not of any significant consequence. If you don't mind, Miss Montorto, I'd prefer we get back on track...I must say, I've not heard any of Brink Town's citizenry reference any little, green men, let alone their adversaries." He turned to Good. "You may have placed some stock in Miss Montorto's claims, but I doubt you'd have made the trip unless there was something more to it...something at least more tangible."

"You underestimate our intuitive intent, Mister Mansford," said Good, at which point the scientists huddled, whispering in German. "When we confirmed the little creatures' existence, we initiated a humanitarian effort to aid them. Nothing wrong with that."

Nothing wrong, indeed, thought Mansford, though the chattering seemed to say otherwise, and through the remnants of his celestial cognition, he absorbed their voices:

"...*How can we tell him when we don't understand ourselves...It took such effort to build the machines, but if the professor were here...Oh, yes, the professor would know what to say, what to do...The professor invented the ghastly devices... The professor knows how they conjured the creatures' chemical compounds... Only the professor can tell this strange man what these specimens really are, why they came to be...The professor does know...doesn't he?*"

"Professor?" Mansford asked, his voice loud and clear. "Who is this professor?"

The scientists pulled away, quivering as Good cleared his throat and then stated, "They're referring to Professor Tarr...Professor Raimond Tarr. He's the genius behind the devices, the one who, for a lack of a better term, understands."

"Do tell," said Mansford. "So, where is he now?"

"On his way," said Good, "from Germany. In fact, his plane arrives at the Chesterville Airport this afternoon. He would have come sooner, but was indisposed on an assignment for the Fuhrer, but his loyalty is a front. The professor's interests, his passions lie elsewhere, particularly with SIIS, which

...reached out and brushed back Montorto's hair...

he has been most instrumental in nurturing. In fact, he's been adamant that its influence gain dominance on American soil, in the land where alleged open-mindedness prevails."

"In other words," said Mansford with a wry grin, "you're saying he's someone I can trust."

"I'm saying," said Good, "this man will give you the answers you seek, the whole ball of wax, as it were."

"Yes," said Montorto, her expression hopeful, her rising bosom accentuating the fact, "he's a most knowledgeable man, yet humble, sincere...willing."

Mansford pulled his eyes from her breasts. "He probably wears scuffed shoes, shabby clothes: the guise of the common man." He shook his head. "I've been down that path before. Nonetheless, the Persona should have no trouble accessing where the professor stands."

"You're welcome to ride with us to the airport," Good offered. "You can meet Professor Tarr as soon as he steps off the plane." He glanced at his watch. "It'll only take a couple hours. The professor would otherwise go straight here via cab. I gave him a key to Miss Montorto's home when I last visited Germany, but I'm sure a face-to-face greeting would please him tremendously." Good paused and grinned. "For what it's worth, he does know of you, Mister Mansford, far more than you might suspect."

"Lovely," said Mansford, unimpressed, "but of course, the Persona has become known in many places, even those well beyond Brink Town. In any event, I'll accept your offer, but only on one condition."

"But of course," said Good. "What might it be?"

He turned to Father Bruno. "You let my friend go. There's no need to keep him."

"A reasonable request," Good consented and clapped, prompting the henchmen to step toward Father Bruno. "My men will be happy to escort—"

Father Bruno leapt away from them. "Sorry, but I'm not going anywhere with those goons."

"It's all right, Father," said Good, waving the men back. "I understand your position. I'll have another set of my recruits assist you."

Father Bruno pressed close to Mansford and whispered, "I recognize the basic locale, Michael. I know where I am. There's a bus stop a mile down the road. I don't mind the walk or the wait. Better that than—"

"If you'd prefer the long hike," Good concluded, "Then so be it. Please—no one's holding you."

Mansford scoped the area, the wary faces, Montorto's included. "I'll walk him part of the way, if you don't mind," he said. "It's the very least I can do, considering the ordeal he's been put through."

With a chuckle, Good threw up his hands and gestured them onward. "As you wish, Mister Mansford...as you wish."

Manford grabbed the father's arm and led him to the door. Once there, he flung it open, letting the priest exit, turning just enough to note Good's beaming smirk among the chilly scowls.

Mansford stepped outside, slamming the door behind them. He then tugged Father Bruno near, as they descended the steps.

"I really hope you've the energy for the haul, Father."

"Don't worry, Michael," the priest assured him, "I'll be fine. I'm more concerned about you." He glanced back. "You could dart for it now, you know, activate your powers, zoom right out of here."

"That would be too easy," said Mansford. "I need a little more time to figure this out." He accompanied the father to the road. "I really do want to meet this professor, see what makes him tick. Let's face it, there's much to inspect right within the vicinity. If I can just move fast enough when the moment comes, reach out with my mind, who knows what I'll find?"

"Sure Michael, I understand." He paused and pouted. "Will I forget Michael...forget again, that is? I really don't like forgetting. It only makes it all the harder when I must remember again, you see."

Mansford smiled. "I'm not sure, Father. I've no control over that department, but if you do retain any details—and I sure hope you do—maybe you can touch base with some of the others, like Carl, Ned and Jack. Perhaps one of them might come up with something useful, but above all, you be careful. Get yourself home nice and safe, all right?"

"No problem, son. God willing, I'll do whatever I can for the cause. I promise you that much."

The priest glanced at the house, saw the blinds sway, faces peering out, including Good's.

He was about to mention such to Mansford, but saw the ethereal way his friend's jacket wavered, his deepening stare and figured it best to let things be. Without further word, he headed down the road.

When he looked back, he saw Mansford marching away from the house, his movements swift yet trance-like. He was on a mission for sure, but to where and what, the priest could only speculate.

• • •

The smoky presence appeared, in a coat as brown as the tree by which it stood, with a tie as green as its leaves.

With a sideways glance, Mansford acknowledged the saint, but uttered not a peep, for he needed more time to think.

"I see you've found the lower, front panel," Surrogate remarked.

"I peered through the steel," Mansford gave in with an agitated sigh, "then triggered it open through sheer will—and without the full activation of the Persona." He knelt. "There's some sort of lens inside…a camera, but for the life of me, I can't make head nor tails of its purpose."

"Interesting," said the saint. "I'd say, the panel isn't regular steel, any more than the lens is of a common variation, but the parts do seem to work accordingly. Each machine is geared the same way and for the same purpose. Naturally, the SIIS scientists are documenting whatever causes and effects manifest."

"Appreciate the scoop," said Mansford, surprised Surrogate offered as much as he did. He stood and with folded his arms, turned to his mentor. "Anything else you'd like to add?"

"You'd have deciphered the basic gist soon enough," Surrogate replied, "and on your own accord, you'll figure out the rest." He pointed in the house's direction. "They're not threatened by your snooping. In fact, they've anticipated it."

"Yes," said Mansford, "Nice to know."

"I don't have every answer," the saint explained, "but I offer what tidbits I can in the limited time I have. The Lord works in mysterious ways, as you know, and the game of life is wrought with obstacles and calamity. Those of us who persevere will come to understand the master plan and in the end—"

"Please," Mansford snapped, "spare me the righteous philosophy. At least tell me, though, whether I have cause for concern. Is this phenomenon Guaner connected?"

The saint frowned. "By no means directly. This manifestation is spawned from the same metaphysical principles, with the same sort of dimensional rifts occurring at simultaneous points—Guaner inspired, yes—but it's still only an impression of what you encountered prior. This is more of an accidental occurrence that's been reformulated, if you will. However, whether it's designed for better or worse, that's up for debate."

"Ambiguous, Surrogate, but why would I expect otherwise." Mansford again regarded the machine and shook his head. "All the same, ambiguous or not, I do believe I can crack this nut."

"For now, you may find yourself blocked from that," the saint warned. "A perplexing force permeates this area, nurtured by the SIIS collective. They may not be Christian, but they do know how to pray in their own way. Results, though misguided, do occur as such, especially when properly guided. Even the Persona will wrestle with the results. It's like a mental wave that's been dispatched and now moves of its own accord."

"Why make such a thing?" Mansford asked. "As the Persona, I slapped Montorto down pretty easily. The SIIS members may have their varying powers, but she's the only one who could have accomplished such a feat, but again, she has limitations."

"Perhaps," speculated the saint. "It could be, too, that a fair sum of the lady's strength was extinguished before the Persona intervened. Keep in mind, even the strongest pugilist will weaken in later rounds. If she…along with Good and select others…planted a lingering layer of blockage prior to the machines' activation, then perhaps, she can take the brunt of the blame, but don't discount any possibility. There's much more to come."

"Professor Tarr," said Mansford. "I know."

Murmurs rose in the distance, followed by a light thud of feet.

"They're coming," said Surrogate, "but they'll be pleased as punch you're giving it your all. Indeed, the professor may very well yet hold an even more significant key to this than Montorto." He waved his hand over his face, and smoke encircled it. "As always, I'll be hovering nearby, watching…listening." His body began to fade, and he merged with the escalating breeze. "Good luck, my dear protégé. Till we meet again."

Good was first to appear before the clearing, the scientists queued from behind, then the band mates, the two henchmen, and Montorto at the far left. She cuddled herself, conveying she knew she had been exposed and wished no further uncovering.

"Were you speaking to someone?" asked Good, looking from side-to-side. "I heard a voice, thought I saw a man, brown-suited, as it were."

"It must have been a trick of the wind," said Mansford and kicked the panel shut. "Sorry, but I felt the urge to look about. Hope you don't mind my returning to the scene."

"No, no," said Good, "you're more than welcome to investigate." He glanced at the closed panel. "So, any conclusions?"

"None of immediate importance," said Mansford. "Did you expect me to find something?"

Good laughed. "Not really. Perhaps after you and Professor Tarr converse, you'll gain a better handle." He tapped his wrist. "Actually, why linger? Let's head to the airport now." He turned around, looked to the left and waved.

"Miss Montorto, please, if you don't mind…"

"I wouldn't have it any other way," Montorto quipped.

Good clapped. "There we have it, then." He spun and stretched. "The rest of you may disperse, but be on call, in the event an impromptu meeting is required. Despite the various snags involved, at least you witnessed today's most profound, paranormal event. You have my unswerving admiration and respect." He placed his hands upon his chest. "Indeed, thank you all."

The members sauntered away, the scientists mumbling, the henchmen grumbling, the band mates shrugging, all moving toward their vehicles. Good and Montorto edged toward Mansford and waited for the flock to leave.

Their engines revved. The wheels churned, implying that, with nothing left to pursue at this point, they were pleased to embrace Good's granted reprieve.

"Please," said Good, walking toward his black Ford and waving them to follow. "We're about to embark on a most intriguing venture and with ample time to chat, we can get to know one another better."

"If you don't mind," said Mansford, "I'll pass on the idle chatter."

"As you wish," said Good, trying not to look offended. "At the very least, please ride up front with me."

"Miss Montorto can have that honor," said Manford. "I'll opt for the rear." He smirked. "I insist."

Good and Montorto exchanged sour pouts, then with a huff, Good picked up pace. Mansford motioned Montorto to follow her confidant, which she obliged with a huff of her own.

Mansford followed at a leisurely pace, watching Good open the door, allowing Montorto to slink into the passenger side. Then with a click and skip, Good leapt inside, wasting no time to start the engine, coincidentally clicking the radio to Mansford's favorite classical-music station as he entered…

As they rolled onward, Mansford's gaze grew clearer, his awareness more acute, if only to ensure no unexpected turn occurred along the way.

VII

T he sun was big and warm by noon, creating an overpowering glare through the windshield, but clouds fast approached, threatening rain, and then there was the plane.

"Ah, yes," cooed Good, as he entered the airport lot, "fate has dealt the cards in our favor." He glanced at Montorto and pointed up. "Impeccable timing."

Montorto looked, as Good careened into a spot. "How do you know it's him?" she asked, pressing her brow against the glass. "That's surely not his plane...is it?"

Good chuckled. "Oh, 'ye of little faith'... You surely sense his presence, my dear."

The Matthew reference intrigued Mansford, and he wondered if his surrogate saint was listening, what might he think?

Montorto sighed. "Yes, I do sense him—sense him quite clearly, in fact."

Good turned off the engine and glanced back at Mansford. "So, ready to meet the maestro?"

"Maestro?" Mansford rolled his eyes. "Quite the high-brow designation, wouldn't you say?"

Good did not elaborate and mirthfully leapt out, darting to the passenger's side to let Montorto out. The sky then darkened, and the rain fell hard.

Mansford exited, as Montorto shielded her head, poising herself toward a white-washed building, atop which a large, painted sign, with sun-bleached bi-planes read: CHESTERVILLE AVIATORS GRILL ... JAVA ... SANDWICHES ... SOUP.

"Don't fret, my dear," Good said. "A little rain surely won't hurt us now, will it? We'll get a bite after we greet the professor."

Mansford let Montorto accompany Good's brisk lead, focusing on the long-propellered, black plane that rolled onto the runway, the haunting sky arching over it, streaked with remnants of faint sunrays and purplish streaks which seemed more akin to late dusk than early afternoon.

The plane stopped and, in a matter of seconds, a set of black, steel stairs cranked from its side, as a moon-face, goggled pilot glanced at the trio from his angled window. Then at the threshold, a booted form emerged, projecting a tall, thin frame, fixed in a long, leather coat.

"Here, here," Good said with a click. "There's our man of the hour—our dear, prestigious Professor Raimond Tarr."

"Hans," the shadow exclaimed and with great grace, descended, his boots refracting what sunny specks yet prevailed, while his face beamed an uncanny, pretty-boy world-weariness: high cheekbones and brow, with hair long and sandy, tucked back behind his small, circular ears, his eyebrows groomed to match his curled mustache and Conquistador goatee. "Wonderful to see you, my faithful friend." He touched ground and widened his arms. "Come—come here."

His accent was indistinguishable, even if his eccentric mode conveyed foreign origin. When he embraced Good, he did so with such force to cause the man to cough. He then released Good with an abrupt thrust and with wide-eye jubilance, scanned his face.

"It's so gratifying to touch the U.S.," he said, "so good to see my good friend... my dear Mister Good." He laughed and then looked at Montorto. "But no lovelier sight could there be than that of the insightful Miss Montorto."

Montorto curtsied and blushed. "Thank you, Professor Tarr."

"For once, my dear," the professor said, stepping past Good, "let's drop the formality. It's Raimond." He extended his arms. "Raimond...yes?"

"Yes, Raimond," she breathed, allowing him to lift her off her feet. "Oh my, your grip—it's a smidgeon strong, I fear."

"Forgive me," the professor said, setting her down. "I couldn't help myself." He peered into her eyes. "What's this? Why...I sense you're not well."

"It's nothing," she said, "a mere headache. It'll pass once I have something to eat."

Mansford cleared his throat, making Tarr glance his way.

Much to Montorto's dismay, the professor inched away, turning upon his heels. To Mansford, he said, "And so here you are—the mythic mystic, no less...ersatz, Michael Mansford." He extended his hand. "I'm Doctor Raimond Tarr...your friendly Nomadic Professor of Paranormal Studies." He emitted a Good-like click of his heels. "Honored to meet you, sir."

Mansford regarded the professor's pale fingers before accepting them; then shook as the rain thickened.

"To the eatery," Good wailed, charging onward. "Hurry, now, hurry."

Though Montorto and Good shot through the budding puddles, Mansford and the professor paused, their eyes locked, the latter smiling, the former stoic. They tried hard—perhaps too much so—to probe each other's thoughts, but the drumming rain proved a distraction, making the professor blink.

In shame, Tarr turned to the plane and raised his arm. The pilot, now positioned at the doorway, nodded and pressed his palm against its inner edge. A mechanical whirr emerged, along with the stairs, which cranked upward, leveling a notch below the lower cusp, flattening like a set of fallen dominos as it slid inward.

The professor dropped his arm and made a slight wave. The pilot waved back and pressed his other palm against the opposite edge, causing the door to swoosh shut.

Mansford noticed, painted on the door in lurid green and smudged in flecks of purple, a small, naked creature, leaping sideways into the air, limber limbs stretched, fingers and toes spread. It resembled Sontar, and its impression magnified Mansford's suspicion and dread.

"Ah, technology," said Tarr, with a loving purr, the rain funneling around his ears, slickening his outer locks. "It's rather like magic, and what would our lives be without magic, eh, Mister Mansford?"

Mansford smiled in response. He then yanked up his collar and turned, proceeding to the restaurant, as Good and Montorto made their way in, his pace not too fast, not too slow, calculated only enough to space himself ahead of the professor.

Mansford—or more rather, his spiritual counterpart—felt no reason to distrust this man, but neither one to embrace him: a perplexing situation, which he soon hoped to remedy.

• • •

"Got more towels at the counter," the burly, aproned man said.

"I'm fine," said Good, tossing one back to the gent. "And you, Melody? Another to dab your hair?"

Montorto shook her head and returned hers also to the man, then adjusted her long legs beneath the small, corner table.

The owner glanced at Mansford and Tarr, who had slipped into their chairs: Mansford alongside Montorto and Tarr alongside Good, the professor and mystic facing each other, eyes once more fixed.

"Uh, don't suppose you fellows want a towel," said the owner.

After an awkward pause, Good answered for them. "Thank you, my good man. I believe they'll make due."

"Okay," the man replied. "Be back with the menus...unless you already know what you're havin'."

"I'll take tea with lemon," said Montorto and glanced at the small blackboard propped behind the counter, listing the day's specials, "and a chicken-salad sandwich...with lettuce." She then winced, rubbed her temple. "Oh, and would you happen to have some aspirin?"

"In the back," said the man, giving her bosom a conspicuous glance. "I'll getcha some."

"Coffee—black—for me," Good interjected, unnerved by the continuing staring match, "and perhaps some for these gents...please."

With a roll of his eyes, the man stomped away, as the sputtering rumble of the departing plane could be heard from outside.

The staring stopped, with both Mansford and Tarr glancing toward the rain-streaked window, watching the plane ascend into flight.

"How wonderful, Raimond," said Good, grateful for the interruption. "I'm pleased you plan to stay for more than the designated day."

Tarr smiled. "Yes, why shouldn't I, Hans? With my various assignments temporarily on hold, I've now time to indulge in what matters."

"So," said Mansford, "there are matters actually more important than those of the Fatherland?"

Tarr's smile faded.

Good stirred. "I mentioned your activities to Mister Mansford in passing," he said, "and also explained that—"

Tarr raised his hand, silencing his friend and again met Mansford's gaze.

"The concern would be otherwise warranted," the professor explained with a serendipitous air, his stare sharpening, "and yet Mister Mansford, you should have enough sense to know, I am not the enemy."

Mansford did not wish to reveal his lack of full penetration, especially since he sensed Tarr was an expert at blockage. He also realized that Montorto, despite her headache, was abetting the eccentric. In fact, when the burly man returned with Montorto's tea and aspirin, her sense of relief—and the flow of her mental pulsations—peaked.

"What are you trying to hide, professor?" asked Mansford, hoping to stall. "I wish I could say otherwise, but I do sense some element of deceit."

Montorto stiffened, and her mental flow tottered.

"Your sandwich is on the way, miss," said the owner, capping the aspirin bottle. "I'll be right back with the coffee."

"I'm not hiding anything," said Tarr, though his expression became strained. "I'm readily available to you." He tapped his forehead. "You only need knock, and the door shall be open."

"Yes," iterated Montorto, her pulsations now cascading behind Mansford's neck. "Open the door, Mister Mansford, and indeed, you shall see."

Her claim, however, was quite the contrary, only increasing Mansford's ire and from such, granting him just enough thrust to break Tarr's shield.

"What…what was that?" Montorto squawked, her brainwaves dipping. She glared at Mansford. "What did you do?" She turned to Tarr whose face had softened like pale putty. "Oh, my…you've…you've cut through. You…you can see inside."

"*Yes, I can,*" said Mansford, his telepathic tone drawled but firm as it encompassed the table. "*I can see quite a bit, at that.*"

In a flash, he envisioned Tarr's fingers skimming a series of pages, flipping them—familiar pages featuring German text that, in Mansford's intensified mode—looked like the old Guaner passages he had once absorbed, but this particular document was crisper, far better preserved, and the sections spoke of specialized portals deep and unique. They also described, albeit in cryptic terms, how to teleport oneself in such a way that the designated locales could become as if one.

"I must learn—must understand," Mansford declared, the mask now flush against his skin. "How exactly do these monsters, these ancient Guaners, do it? Is it through science, magic, a bit of trickery…or all of the above?"

He felt the professor's brain brim with mystical aspirations, with ideas swarming from his dreams, egging him on until, within the man's frustrated reverie, he stood like some pompous director at the onset of a production, undaunted by the steamy, old, brick-and-mortar shop in which his superiors had stationed him, with black-smocked subordinates scuttling about, drafting plans, soldering sheets of steel, placing large, silver spheres atop them, then by his precise command, pulling levers and clicking switches.

Thunderclaps and flashes bright and blinding came and passed. The air burned, and inside the purple smoke, things budged, clawed, tried to wiggle their way out, but to succeed, they needed form, more thoughts and patterns upon which to attach. There was no question that this design acted as a platform for such: a means with which portions of fantasy could become reality.

The subordinates skidded about, whimpering and clasping their ears, due to the grand prototype's obstreperous hums, waiting for an inevitable explosion, but much to their gratified dismay, all stayed smooth and easy, for the professor had harnessed a spreading plasmatic stream via his thoughts, grabbing the machine's spewing purple mist and expanding it. Within its strange heart, he grasped the seeds from which he could now make life, but how might it be textured, how big in scale, how small?

The Persona sensed the professor's recollection of the fairy creatures from his youth: goblins, leprechauns…trolls, their pigments smooth and livid, envious green, their bodies adorned by fuzzy fabric, makeshift armor and in their spindly, little hands, piercing weapons.

He saw their bodily fluids encompass the prismatic molds he had erected, which became like floating frescos, bobbing about, inundating the indentations like gooey rubber, the content at first flaccid, but then with a magnanimous nudge of his mind, bringing forth beating hearts and crooked mouths, eyes beady and bulging.

"Breathe," he bellowed, "breathe…breathe…breathe."

Though their chests heaved, the words failed to resonate, and so they withered inside their translucent compartments, their artificial flesh dissipating, fading to yellow-green drops, which pelted the floor. The machine rumbled in despair, spewing more purple smoke and fiery sparks, churning such blistering heat that before long, the figures (along with the translucent outlines that hoisted them) could no longer sustain the cataclysmic torment and as such, burst from sight.

Oh, what a horrible failure. What a sinful shame. To come so close, only now to be so far? What was Tarr to do?

Melancholy seized the professor. He felt the days pass, dipped in despair, but as he wallowed in his dark office, a letter came, post-marked U.S.A. It was from Herr Gut's lovely protégé, Miss Melody Montorto, who claimed that something interesting yet disquieting had transpired in the field across her home: a phenomenon, in fact, reflected aspects of his experiments.

Her letter implied how the very fabric of reality had dissolved, and in its aftermath, she had become plagued by nightmares so succinct that she feared she might never wake from them, for they held large, controlling, multi-limbed beasts with hypnotic charms, some of whom could even disguise themselves as men. She said she doubted anything so bizarre could be real, but try as she may to disbelieve, her overriding psyche accepted the visions. She had no doubt, the demons were real.

"Stop, stop, stop," Montorto screamed, pounding her fists on the table, making Mansford and Tarr snap from their trance. "I don't want to see any more of those ugly things." She regarded Mansford with teary eyes. "What the SIIS membership is conducting…it…it isn't the same." She then looked to Tarr and sobbed, "Please, Raimond, make him understand. Make him see—really see—before he does something rash. Just look at his face. Traces of your own features cling to the mask. He'll use such tactics against you—against us."

Poof! The masked dropped, and Mansford rubbed his face, smoothing away any remaining imprint of Tarr. The owner slid a cup before Mansford, and into it, he stared, murmuring, "You should be cautious of your experimentation, Doctor Tarr. Nothing good can come from the Guaners. By its very nature, their technology…if you can call it that…is flawed."

Tarr took a deep breath and with all his might, refocused. "But I did control it," he argued, rapping the table as sweat seeped from his vein-creased brow. "I manipulated it to my own design, my purest impulses, and with uncanny precision. No matter what it may have looked like, what sprung from such was honorable and good because…because, my dear Mister Mansford, I am a benevolent artist, you see, a considerate creator. Say what you will about the Guaners, but a good man can only conjure good."

Mansford winced. "So, you fancy yourself a god with the SIIS members, the apparent disciples of your new religion. This would explain the music—a band playing an adopted hymn of homage of the purple onset…and yes, the tension rose, an impulsive gyration to cap the holy moment. Hallelujah, praise the new

"Stop, stop, stop!" Montorto screamed.

lord! You even staged the proceedings within a rented nightclub, a temporary church, with a cleric and mystic of a different faith, just happening to invade your sacred space."

"I don't know what you're saying," Tarr scoffed, finding it hard to conceal his lie, but Good reached over, whispered into the professor's ear, and when the scholar had heard enough, he said to Mansford, "All right, you make a valid point. What has transpired is, in a manner of speaking, sacred to us. It would only go to reason that, at least in an off-the-cuff way, we would emulate some religious practices. That doesn't constitute our beliefs as an actual religious doctrine or make us some new-fangled cult, but even if such were the case, why assume it bad?"

"If King Sontar and his merry men are benign," Mansford deduced, "fine, but you surely can't say that of their adversaries? They're also the result of your thoughts…your emotions…correct?"

Tarr groaned. "Lurking behind every Jekyll, there resides a Hyde," he said, one side of his mouth twitching upward, the other down. "I'm well aware of my experiments' consequences. However, a few incidental weeds will not spoil a garden. Weeds only need to be extracted. Once that's done, a better world can take root, and from it, we can learn so much. Think of it—a world devoid of outside influence, allowed to flourish as might the fabled Garden of Eden, but without end and open to all. If we take our time to study the results of such phenomenon, perhaps we might even crack the code of life—even gain some insight on how the human race came to be. The potential outcomes would be nothing short of astounding."

"I see," said Mansford, "However, to understand your theories, I must better understand you." He looked to Good and then Montorto. "I must understand each of you, in fact. You're each part of this set-up and what makes it tick. I'll admit, what's developed probably extends well beyond any Guaner influence, but that a Guaner aspect prevails at its core, disturbs me greatly, as does this evident Nazi link." He glared at Tarr. "Really, how can I not think there's some insidious cause at play? Who's all this for, Professor…you…your followers… dear Adolf?"

"My connection to the Fatherland," explained Tarr, "is more incidental than planned. I only ever offered the bastards a little, clever, carnival fortune-telling, but I assure you, Mister Mansford, my allegiance lies elsewhere."

"A double agent?" asked Mansford.

"Oh, I'm much more than a two-faced spy," said Tarr. "I'm my own man, working for my own interests and of course, those of SIIS." He swung his finger from Good to Montorto, who nibbled nervously of her sandwich. "As for this particular phenomenon, it was launched at non-German ground, with the resulting manifestations adopting the locale's indigenous characteristics. I would never wish such variables tarnished by those who lust for conquest. For that very same reason, I also desire the larger, incidental specimens expelled, leaving only the smaller ones to prevail." He grabbed a napkin, padded his temple. "It's as basic as that."

Mansford sipped his coffee, in hopes the pause might spur Tarr to reveal more.

"I'll…I'll show you how the process works," the professor offered. "We can disassemble one of the machines, reveal the extent of its inner workings, and from there, you can decide. So, what do you say? Have we a deal?"

Good leaned over. "You should be honored, Mister Mansford. The professor rarely shares with just anyone."

"Indeed," said Tarr, offering Mansford his hand.

Mansford took another sip of coffee, glanced at Good, then Montorto, who had just finished her tea. She smiled, her vibes beaming, but without threat of penetration.

Mansford slipped his hand into the professor's and this time fastened tight.

Tarr chuckled as they shook. "Excellent, Mister Mansford, excellent."

Mansford grinned, but then wrenched his hand free, warning all three, "This will be your last shot, though. Truly, my patience is waning. Am I understood?"

Good glanced away; Montorto fluttered her lashes. Tarr nodded and said, "Understood. You'll have no regrets, Mister Mansford. I assure you that."

With this, there was little more to say or do, beyond pay the check, which Mansford did before they could object, and back into the mist they trekked, Tarr seated upfront; Mansford and Montorto in the rear.

"The workhouse?" Good asked Tarr.

"Of course," said the professor. "Better there, I'd say, than the field." He glanced back at Mansford. "Most of the machinery and their various parts are stored there. You'll appreciate that—nothing concealed."

Mansford nodded, and Montorto eased her way nearer.

"Maybe this will convince you," she whispered. "Maybe this will finally make you…well, see."

Mansford averted her gaze.

Beyond the airport they then traveled, the sky lightening, its clouds fading to reveal lingering, purple streaks throughout, like Montorto, Mansford thought: beautiful, but foreboding.

IX

"That's right," Father Bruno insisted. "That's where I want to get off."

"I thought you said the orphanage," the bus driver barked. "This is the gag shop. Besides, you'll be well off the trail, and if the weather shifts again..."

"I'll be fine," the priest retorted, well aware of the impatient passengers watching hm. He waddled toward the exit. "Please, sir, let me off."

"Okay," the driver consented. "If that's what you want, padre..."

No sooner had the door opened, Father Bruno leapt out, glancing up at the big clown face on the ESOTERIC INCORPORATED sign above. The buffoonish countenance unsettled him, and he had no desire for frivolity.

He marched straight toward the entrance, as the bus, with a disdainful swoosh, barreled onward, oblivious to the shiny limo that was parked along the side and the old, smiling chauffeur within.

"Hey, Father," the driver called, rolling down the window, tipping a size-too-small cap. "Father—it's Charlie. Remember? I used to work at Mister Mansford's hotel."

Father Bruno didn't catch much of what the man said, except "remember." Remember what exactly? For that matter, why had he felt the urge to come here? Nonetheless, for whatever odd reason, he knew he had to chat with Ned Stark.

Yes, as silly as it seemed, Stark's face had entered his head somewhere along the ride, and not because he knew Esoteric was up ahead. Other faces, in fact, had also risen: Carl Clive, Jack Murphy, Phil Sutton, Mayor Poindexter...heck, even garrulous Charlie, the hotel guard. Wait—was that him in the limo?

No matter. He had to push on, or so that's what impulse dictated.

He strutted into the building and charged down the hall, where zigzagging employees greeted him with respectful glances and nods.

"Ned Stark—where's his office?" he asked a pimply-faced lass.

"Right down the hall," she said. "Keep going. You'll see—says PROTOTYPES on the door." She smiled. "You've an appointment, father?"

"No," said the priest, rushing onward, "but thanks, my dear. I may not have an appointment, but that shouldn't make my business any less important."

Now, if only he knew what that business was. Well, whatever the case, he was sure it would all come clear when he was in Stark's presence.

He spotted the cardboard sign on the door, knocked a couple times, and when there was no answer, decided just to enter.

Stacks of boxes flanked him, marked by sloppy handwriting: JOY BUZZERS… WHOOPEE CUSHIONS…CLUTCHING HANDS. He bounced among them, squeezing his way through the musty maze.

"Ned," he shouted. "Ned Stark…you here? It's Father Bruno…Father Bruno from the orphanage. Ned…Ned…I need to see you."

He heard some murmurs, then Ned shouted, "Hey, friend. We're in the back, near the window. Just follow the trail."

Was he in a meeting? Great… However, when he stumbled his way toward the work desk, he not only saw Stark behind it, but around it were familiar faces: Clive, Murphy, Sutton and lo and behold, Mayor Percival Poindexter, no less, all decked out in his spiffy, pinstriped suit and silver tie.

"Whoa—hello there, Father," the mayor chimed. "We were wondering when you'd show. It seems we've been guided by the same strange, elusive thing."

"An insatiable need to talk," added Stark, looking grave, "and maybe a few odd memories along the way. As I said to the others, I'm flattered the guys picked this as the meeting spot…or is it more a starting point? You got me. Too bad Mike isn't here. Something tells me he's the point of interest, with this being his main stomping ground and all." He picked a rubber rat off the table, accidentally squeezed it and then tossed it to the side. "Whether he's the catalyst or not—and how could he not be?—something weird… and undoubtedly big…is sure brewing. No doubt of that."

"You mean, like before?" Sutton said, his face wrought with remembrance. "Hot diggity. So, does that mean it wasn't just a dream? Still, I wouldn't think we need a damn sequel."

"Wait," Father Bruno interjected. "Maybe I can assist. I left Michael a short while ago with some rather peculiar types, and in that regard, yes, something weird…and big…is brewing, but as to what precisely, I can't rightly say." He paused and rubbed his beard. "I fear it might be an offshoot of what happened before…Guaner based—that's what they're called, right…Guaners? Anyway, that's the only thing that makes sense to me. It was the Guaner rise that linked us, and this strange troupe wishes to form some sort of alliance with Michael… or that is, the Persona…to help with their for their cause."

"Come again?" Murphy said, tapping his holster. "So, are these characters anything like that Ben Gyler crowd?"

A silence fell over the room, and into their subconscious reservoirs they plunged, each sharing images of that fateful, summer night, of the multi-limbed creatures and fake, fickle men. They recalled how the Persona had ascended like an avenging angel to dispatch the cretins, but only with their combined, heartfelt help. Together, they had become a force to reckon with and believed they could become such again. Still, they had to ascertain who these new people were and if need be, how to combat them.

"I say they're different than Gyler's gang," Father Bruno said. "The same goes for the creatures involved—spanking new entities, big and small...all from some other dimension."

His tone was perhaps more Mansford's than his own, even teetering on the Persona's, and he was proud to stand by every word.

They contemplated the information, but became distracted when the door opened. Scuttling feet and panting followed. Then they saw Charlie heading toward them.

"Sorry, Mister Mayor...sorry Mister Stark," he huffed, "but I couldn't help myself. Just felt compelled to touch base." He shook his head, knocking the sweat off, much to Poindexter's disdain. "All of a sudden, it came back to me, strong and clear, more than memories, more than any dream." He removed his cap, fanned his face. "We're sure in the thick of it, aren't we? I'm talkin' big-time thick, too...and even more perplexing than before."

"I told you he was part of this," Sutton growled at the mayor. "When we get snobbish and distance folks, we only hurt ourselves. I'll say, you've sure gotten big for your britches, Percy. Bet you even skimp on the poor guy's salary."

"Don't be ridiculous," the mayor scoffed. "I had Charles park out front in the event we had to make a fast getaway. I mean, really, there's no question danger's in the air."

"Aw, don't worry about it, Mister Mayor," Charlie said. "It's all fine and dandy. I get paid well, do what I'm told. I'm not one to argue, not one to question, unless it's something of a higher magnitude. Then, gosh, I got no choice."

"Let's cut the sweet talk," said Sutton, "and get down to business. Mike's got the damn blessing when it comes to this metaphysical stuff. The rest of us are just foot soldiers...you, too, Percy. The thing is, without Mike here, what do we do? I mean, we're here for a reason, but what is it? We don't seem to be accomplishing anything. That makes me nervous."

"Well, arguing isn't going to help the matter," said Poindexter.

"Who's arguing," asked Sutton. "Heck, I'm not arguing." He looked to the others. "Am I arguing?"

"Enough already," said Stark. "We've got to come to terms with this—period."

"Ned's right," said Murphy. "We've got to come up with some plan of action, based on what we know." He looked at the priest. "Right, father?"

Father Bruno nodded, searching for some further insight, but all in vain.

"You said Mike is with these...these characters," Murphy continued, "that they're seeking some sort of pact with him. I take it, though, they're shady… can't be trusted."

"That's my gut feeling," confirmed the father. "I think it's safe to say we're all of the same inclination."

There came another moment of unsteady silence, another pensive ascent, into which flickers of the little, green men and their brawny assailants crossed their collective consciousness. They all cringed.

Poindexter cleared his throat. "I say, we all have a solid notion of where to go."

"Yeah," said Murphy, "the field."

"Near that old home we visited," Sutton added, "where that sultry dame lives. "

"It's easy enough to get to," said Murphy.

"Yeah," said Stark, "real easy."

Clive tapped his temple. "It's refreshing what a united mind can achieve, isn't it?"

"There's ample room in the limo for us," Poindexter suggested, heading for the closest makeshift aisle. "Charlie will drive."

"You got that right, Mister Mayor…sure will. Anything for an important cause, I say, and if ever there was an important cause, this is it. By golly, there's good reason why we're all on the same visionary path here, and if it were otherwise—"

"Okay, Charlie, okay" the mayor blustered. "We got the idea."

Father Bruno, ignited by the enthusiasm, began to budge, but then hesitated. "Not everyone's here…and I don't mean Michael." His words struck a nerve. "Miss Standish—she should be part of this. Why isn't she?"

The others strained their collective consciousness until the answer came, and then in one fell swoop, barreled onward.

X

 "Stacey," the usher called. "Stacey, where are you?"

The young man's voice droned in her head, stirring her from her spot beneath the sink. She had grown dizzy and so darted into the employee's bathroom to slap some water on her face. Then things got worse.

Though Standish had never met the woman, Montorto's semblance had surfaced in her head with alarming familiarity: raven hair; smooth, pale skin;

big bosom; long nyloned legs, propped by stilettos.

Standish also sensed Mansford's presence. Was he with this woman and if so, why? Was it to follow through on the letter, or…

Sadness overcame her, and his face grew clearer, edging closer. In a dreamy, detached voice, he muttered, "I was once yours, but now I'm hers. I'm sorry, Stacey, so sorry, but her hold on me has proven too strong. Unfortunately, this is the way it must be. If not, I'd have no means to remedy the calamity, and it must be remedied at all costs."

Surely, these words weren't his. They had to be planted, but by whom?

"Calamity?" she whimpered. "What calamity?"

"Stacey," the usher continued, pounding the door. "Stacey—you in there? Answer me, will yah?"

Mansford's face expanded inside her mind's eye like a moon, growing hard, porcelain-like and then it started to crack, revealing another face beneath: virtually hairless and monocle-rimmed. It snarled at her and then twisted into a gaunt, goateed man, whose eyes sported a mischievous glint. Their names came clear—Gut and Tarr—but then the damned brunette's face resurfaced, harnessing her focus.

"I'm coming in, Stacey," the usher threatened. "I swear—I'm coming in."

Montorto's face was ripe with spite. *Too late,* the woman's eyes conveyed, *Michael Mansford is mine…all mine.*

Stacey sprung up, flailing her fists. "You can't have him," she shrieked. "I won't let you. I won't…"

The usher threw himself against the door: once, twice, and then the door fell inward. Stacey leapt backward, into the wall.

However, she did not see the young man or any of those who rushed in: not the lanky, old owner; the pigtailed popcorn girl; or freckled-face lad who jerked the sodas. She only saw—only heard—Montorto, or at least what was left of her. The vixen's throat whistled like a dissipating kettle, her skin spewing at the center like a collision of clouds: symbolic, disturbing and threatening.

Stacey flailed, knocking off the usher's cap. "No, no—go away," she sobbed. "Go away."

In an abrupt burst of violet stardust, she perceived a group of little, green men leaping about: one cluster after another, each the same in size and design, their members sprinting with their spidery legs, hoisting sharp weapons, while from out a rising, outer twirl of purple, larger green specimens stomped, soon dominating her view.

They were armored, brawny, their incisors bared. They picked up pace, but then slowed, looking upon the masked, ethereal shape that descended upon them: Edwardian garbed, billowing scarf and in his gloved hand, a dagger.

"Michael," she cried. "Michael…"

The usher grabbed Standish's arm; the old gent braced her neck. The girl pressed her legs and whispered, "We knew she had problems…so odd and aloof. Poor thing…"

She watched the Persona dip and felt the wind rise.

She screamed, to the point where the folks had no choice but to release her.

Standish snapped from her stupor: the vision dead, replaced by their startled faces.

"I'm…I'm so sorry," she sobbed, stumbling toward the mirror. "I'm fine now," she choked, fluffing her hair and forcing a silly smile. "I should go now. I…I should—"

"See a doctor," the old man blurted.

"Better yet," said the usher, "I'll take you to the hospital." He looked at the owner. "Mister Sinclair won't mind."

"'Course I won't mind," the old man said, grabbing her hand and patting it. "Here…here…let's get you to Johnny's car."

"No," she protested, pulling free and then between them. "I have to go. I have to—"

She tripped into the hall, then into the lobby, catching the tense looks of concession-counter workers and patrons. She burst through the doors, emitting a long, forlorn moan, before falling onto the pavement.

She heard feet fast approaching, people asking if she was all right. She did not respond, for more visions had invaded her thoughts: a field lush and vast, but enclosed, shielded as if by invisible walls. It was a prison, she decided, and in it stood the smug, monacled man and his gaunt, goateed partner. She peered past them, and much to her dismay, saw her reflected self alongside Mansford and the brooding Montorto reaching toward him, her crimson nails stretched like a wild cat's, ready to graze his chest.

"Get away from him," she yelled. "You can't have him—you hear?" She swatted at the air. "You're not entitled, you…you pompous harlot. I…I won't allow it. I won't—"

Other presences entered, but whether in the vision or outside it, she could not tell. They sliced through the mounting chatter—the voices of Stark, Sutton, Murphy, Poindexter…Father Bruno. Yes, Father Bruno, sounding sharp and regal, pious and strong.

"Keep the faith, my child," the padre said, his face coming into view. "Whatever you do—don't succumb to fear."

He reached down, helped her up.

"Snap out of it, dear," the owner implored.

"Please, Miss Standish," the usher begged. "Wake up. Wake up."

An engine's roar helped clear her head. Montorto faded, along with the rest of the reverie, one piece fading into the next, like raindrops in a puddle. The flanking citizens grew more succinct, their expressions taut and perplexed.

She glanced to the side, caught the limo's black sheen, the driver looking at her through the sun-kissed glass. She recognized him: that talkative gent who worked at Mansford's apartment complex, who now drove the mayor's car. He, like Father Bruno, was here to help her. They had read her mind...would take her away...take her to her man.

The limo's doors opened; men leapt from each side, darting her way.

"Now, now, folks," said the mayor, stepping onto the pavement, "there's no need to fret. We'll take it from here."

Father Bruno handed her over to Murphy, who whispered in her ear, "Hold on, Stacey. It's going to be fine."

"She needs a doctor," the owner persisted.

"The hospital," the usher corrected him, "which is where I was going to take her."

"How noble of you," said the mayor, patting the young man's head and then shot a knowing wink to Stark and Sutton. "The hospital is the most logical course."

Charlie stuck his head out the window and asked, "We headin' out or what, Mister Mayor? Time's a-wastin'. If we don't get moving—"

"All right, Charlie, all right," Poindexter blurted as the men escorted Standish into the back. "Indeed, we'll have her under the proper care in a hop and skip." He clapped with finality and then fluttered his arms, inspiring the crowd to disperse. "Thank you for your concern, my good people. It's most appreciated."

They resumed their spots in the limo and with a rocketed skid, Charlie streaked down the street, leaving the old man and usher, scratching their heads.

"How's she holding up, Father?" Poindexter asked, forcing himself around to take a peek. "I must say, she looked terribly worse for wear back there."

Standish frowned. "I'm fine, Mayor Percy," she said, "perfectly fine." She swiveled her head and regarded the rest of the men, before leaning upon the priest's shoulder and giggled. "If my hunch is right, it appears I'm not the only one who's been struck."

"For sure," said Father Bruno, stroking her arm. "Your mind's clearing... shaking off the visionary effects, though I've a hunch what you experienced was much stronger than any of us."

Another silence spread among them, broken when Standish then whined, "I'm sorry, real sorry, fellows." She rubbed her eyes and sighed. "I couldn't help but get unhinged. I really need to get to Michael."

"That's where we're taking you," Father Bruno assured her, "at least in a roundabout way."

"Yes, sir," Charlie began to chatter, "We'll follow our nose on this one. Nine out of ten times, instinct gets it right, but people don't realize that. A shame, because so many of our problems could be solved if we'd just go by our inherent drive…"

They let Charlie ramble on, his voice droning in sync with the engine's relaxing purr, setting the precise mood for their next bold move…whatever it might be.

XI

"The warehouse," Good announced. "Looks unassuming, but inside, it's chockfull of wonders, as Professor Tarr can readily attest."

Indeed, it did not look like much: big, gray and drab; but Mansford sensed a distinct, mechanized aura within: big and in most likelihood, dangerous if not handled with caution.

"At risk of sounding like a braggart," said Tarr, "Hans is correct, Mister Mansford. The most spectacular advancements await us beyond those doors, and to think these wonders emanate right at the cusp of your cherished Brink Town. You should be proud, sir. After all, we're talking breakthrough technology here: world-altering, in fact."

"And reality-altering," offered Good with devilish delight. "Yes, you'll be most impressed, Mister Mansford…most impressed, indeed."

Good parked alongside the structure's big, wooden doors. "Walter Aaronheim operates the lab," he said. "He's a cantankerous old gent, but also the most innovative, underground scientist working these days—next to Raimond, that is. If he snaps at you, let it go, though I'm sure he'll use restraint in your presence, Mister Mansford."

They exited the car, Montorto swaying to the side, her mental frequency yet circling in Mansford's direction, begging him to take a bite. He had to admire her persistence, but what audacity!

"Ahhh," said Tarr, stretching his arms before the looming structure. "Simple yet grand." He rubbed his hands. "I can't wait to engage in some spirited debate with Walter. Our exchanges always intensify the adrenalin."

"Now, now," said Good, shaking his finger and advancing the doors. "You know how much Walter despises the arcane. It would be wise not to get him riled."

"Precisely," said Tarr, shooting Mansford a roll of the eyes. "That's what makes our conversations so spirited, and when all is said and done, we always come to the same conclusions." He shook his head and laughed. "Never fails."

Mansford was about to follow when something grazed his brow. What had it been? An insect? A tickling breeze?

"Please, wait," Montorto's whispery voice curled into his head. *"There's still time, ample time, to enter that stodgy realm. If you really desire it, we could still consummate…mentally, that is."*

He glared at her, noticing the steadfast pretense of her gaze and kept walking.

"You're making a grave mistake," she persisted. *"The blonde knows nothing of inter-dimensional travel and otherworldly rifts."* Her heels clicked faster. *"A man like you deserves an equal…a soulful match."*

"You were no match for me in the field," Mansford countered, oblivious that others might here. "Thanks, but no thanks, my dear."

"Come…come," Good exclaimed. "This is no time to dilly-dally." He poised to knock. "There's so much to see, so much to learn." He rapped fast and hard upon the doors. "Doctor Aaronheim…Doctor Aaronheim—it's me. It's Hans." He rapped faster, harder. "Walter," he shouted, pronouncing the "w" as a crisp "v," his German accent permeating, "it's me. It's Hans. Open up, will you? Please? Bitte?"

Hurried feet sounded inside, followed by a contemptuous grumbling, capped by a long grunt, and then the doors creaked open, revealing a spray of industrial light and beneath it, a small man in a disheveled, white lab coat.

He flattened the gray tufts upon his ruddy crown, a cigarette dangling from his bluish, bottom lip, and just as he focused on his visitors, he began to cough, becoming too immersed in his spasm to acknowledge them.

Mansford absorbed the man's aura: confused, determined…jilted. These were far from envious traits, and yet a whiff of the man's intellect puffed through, as well his heartfelt conviction to do right.

Without introduction, Mansford extended his hand, which halted the man's coughing.

With a cold squint, he sized Mansford up. "So," he mumbled in an accent a trifle more pronounced than Good's, "I presume you're the new mystic supreme …the one who's supposed to help us gain the edge." For a moment his hand reached for Mansford's, but then he rammed it into his coat pocket and dug in his heels "I've seen your photos in the Brink Town Times. Oh, what prestige money can buy."

Tarr clucked his tongue and approached his colleague, but Aaronheim sidestepped him and moved closer to Mansford.

"I…I apologize for my haste," he said and after a pause, decided to remove his hand. Slowly, he offered it. "I'll befriend a man of questionable prestige any day over some long-haired buffoon with illusions of grandeur." As they shook, he shot Tarr his scornful scowl. "Who do you think you are, anyway…bloody Beethoven…Tarzan, perhaps? Really, Raimond, they don't have barbers in the Fatherland? Oh, and what's with the beard. Still aspiring to be Don Quixote?"

Tarr groaned. "What does my appearance matter? I reprimanded you on this form of disdain before, Herr Doktor."

Aaronheim ignored him, focusing instead on Mansford's face. Mansford, in turn, searched the scientist's eyes, touching his innermost thoughts and as such, tasted other aspects of the man: his fear of being conquered, shackled… killed.

Aaronheim broke bond with several swift blinks and with renewed panache, swept his arm toward the threshold and said, "Let's get on with this."

"Hear, hear," said Tarr, with an impatient snort.

"I second that motion," Good chuckled, following the professor and waving Mansford inside. "Come now, come. You shan't be disappointed, Mister Mansford. You'll see. Oh, yes, sir, you'll see…"

Mansford felt Montorto at his heels, her psychic breath still beating at his neck. As soon as they entered, she slammed the doors shut and hopped to the side, her gaze still glued to him.

Mansford paid her no mind and scoped the surroundings, and impressive they were, with big, capped lights bolted to metal beams and fan-braced walls lined with machines similar to the field's, though smaller and comparatively clunkier: prototypes, no doubt.

In the center of the floor was a cluster of six such devices, positioned toward one another, plugged into several back-wall generators, purring and pulsating. Before them, hoisted by thin wires that stretched from one end of the expanse to the other, were six, three-foot-by-three, glassy, square molds, for all intents and purposes, arranged like floating dominos, inside which Mansford discerned impressions: small, faint and humanoid.

"Sontar," Mansford inferred, "or at least a variation of such."

Aaronheim's eyes widened with respect. Good and Tarr glanced at each

"...they don't have barbers in the Fatherland?"

other, at first appearing defensive, but then grinned and nodded.

"You're most perspective," said Tarr. "You're correct. That is Sontar, or at least the basic format my mind forged for him. I can inundate the mold repeatedly with the machine's help, though since then, the devices have become more of a hindrance than a help. Nevertheless, I never saw the sense in conjuring just one offspring. Why not make a beloved slew?"

"Offspring?" said Mansford. He rubbed his jaw, considering the matter. "Hmmm...I see... Sontar...Son of Tarr. Clever...cute, in fact. "

Aaronheim slapped his knee and laughed. "He knows your pompous style, Raimond. Ah, yes, I'm beginning to like you, Mister Socialite. Maybe you really are as insightful as they claim."

Tarr looked disgruntled. "Enough, Walter. "We didn't invite Mister Mansford here for your flippant remarks." He gestured at the mechanized cluster. "Make yourself useful and increase the power—and get those damn cameras ready." His brow throbbed "Go on—activate them, I said."

"You heard him," Good growled, with a trusty click. "Do it."

With a derisive huff, Aaronheim consented. "All right, all right, if that's what you want, you egomaniacal fools."

The scientist moved toward each bulky base, as if ducking beneath some invisible shield. His fingers snapped fast, like those of a frantic pianist, flinging open the panels, tapping their various interiors. With each touch and tap, the machines whirred louder, burping and glowing, churning a pattern of multi-colored webbing among them, and from such, a deep, purple haze formed.

"What's happening?" Mansford asked, feeling the blistering heat, the spread of smoky tendrils. "Something's wrong." Panic seized him. "I want you to stop it—hear?"

Tarr paid him no heed. "That's the way, Walter." He leapt up, giggling like a school girl. "It's so hard to dislike you when you do your job so well. Wonderful, Walter, wonderful."

Meanwhile, Good skipped backward and with subtle grace reached for Montorto, who at this point, watched the phenomenon in dumbstruck awe.

"Look out," Good cried, hurling her into the crackling center.

She spun within the colorful webbing, as the purple cloud descended. She quivered and blinked as it draped her, her head seeming to vibrate, wavering in synch with the gaseous haze.

Mansford dashed toward her, as the cloud's radius expanded, its weird residue moistening his cheeks.

They then reestablished their mental link, and this time, it not only endured, but strengthened. From Montorto's head, images flowed, and Mansford caught them one-by-one, like fish from a lake, until they formed a swirling collage, full of memories he would not have thought her to harbor.

Within the expanse, he saw Standish's home, on the night the Beguiler had broken into it. He saw her family photos—her false, fickle parents, who had sold their souls to the Devil. The photos faded, eclipsed by Standish's woeful eyes. Tears filled them. She sobbed, gasped, her sorrow lingering, spreading. What in God's name did it mean?

"*She's in danger,*" Montorto explained. "*In fact, she's been in danger for quite some time...and in pain...such immense, intense pain. Fear brings pain, you know...in this case, the result of your presence. How selfish of you. You're more than a mere man. Even in Miss Standish's wildest dreams, she could never comprehend the circumstances in which you've placed her. As I tried to tell you, the poor girl could never match your status, never dare hold her own outside your constant watch. She'd be forever sheltered...coddled. What kind of life would that be so full of emptiness, restrictions?*"

Mansford shook Standish's image away and crushed Montorto's words to the point of numbness, but still her eyes remained on his, their minds interlocked.

"*I can prophesize,*" she insisted, "*see the truth, just like you...and show it to others of our kind, Michael. We can improve each other...improve the SIIS and the organization's impact on any given society...if only you would share...if only you would show me the way. Be my mentor...Be my friend...*" The purple air enveloped her further, seeming to stain her skin. "*Even you have a mentor... one to guide you. I've sensed his presence from the start...feel it even now in the corridors of your mind and in the pit of your heart. Please, I beg you, Michael Mansford...magnanimous Persona.... Bestow upon me the same.*"

Though her plea was enticing, Mansford resisted. The Persona resisted.

The machines rumbled onward. Tarr expanded his focus. Good mounted his devious glee. Aaronheim felt ever more troubled and betrayed.

"Look—look," the scientist cried, despising the tumultuous display unfolding before him. "Everything's turning bright—yes, very bright...and dense...too dense. Mansford knows. The time isn't right, Tarr. It's never been right. Perhaps it never will."

The roof rumbled. The ground quaked.

"Hush, Walter," Tarr snapped. "You're the one who should look—look deep and hard into what's forming here. See the field? See it? It's coming into view...a portal to another place...pushing farther inward. Enjoy its purity, doctor...its power." He laughed as if having heard the most uproarious joke. "Oh me, oh my—our mystical pair is certainly churning it up, making it bigger, higher, deeper than ever before. Glorious—absolutely glorious."

The molds ascended, then dipped and rose again, their wires dancing, waving with little or no impact. From the back of Mansford's mind, the Persona watched the molds' indentations become filled with a rush of gooey green: limbs extending, fingers wiggling, chests heaving. Most remained confined to their hoisted, square sectors, while the fluid of others darkened, seeping into the crevasses, turning an ominous, blubbery green.

The entire warehouse vibrated, causing Good to skip about and collide with Aaronheim, who promptly pushed him away. Tarr, meanwhile, tumbled, but managed to regain his balance, but by then the purple mist had drowned the realm, making it difficult for anyone to see, beyond the Persona and because she yet clung to his celestial aura, Montorto.

The portal stretched like a giant's yawn and in it, the Persona saw the SIIS entourage returning to the field, leaping from their vehicles, pointing about. He saw a long, black car, absorbed the familiar faces within. Was that Mayor Percy on the passenger's side, and in the rear, was that Father Bruno, but who was he comforting? No, it couldn't be, but yes, there she was.

"Stacey," he called, her name slicing through the air. "Stacey..."

Creatures broke their translucent molds, which shattered like glass upon impact with the ground. Their flaccid bodies flew as fast as lightning, soaring into storm's depths, bouncing into any number of spots, as dirt and dust mushroomed high.

"*Please, don't abandon me,*" Montorto pleaded. "*Please, stay with me. I beg you—don't let go.*"

The Persona had no intent of loosening his grasp, though more from confusion than grace. He had no idea where he was going, where any of them were.

The urge to complete his physical guise, to don his mask and grab his dagger grew unbearable, but the violet atmosphere had grown too suffocating, the lure of the brewing portal too invigorating. His consciousness careened outward, snapping apart as if into a million stars, stretching, bending, ending, but then reassembling, as he corralled the consciousnesses around him, which upon his mental gaze, turned dark and somber.

"*Where are we going?*" Montorto asked. "*Tell me, please, tell me.*"

The Persona did not answer—could not answer, as they descended ever deeper into a state of catatonia, with the others following, as limp and despondent.

XII

"It appears we've been beaten to the punch," remarked Poindexter, as Charlie parked along the brush.

"What do you mean?" asked Father Bruno, trying hard to see through the windshield's glare, catching the SIIS congregation as it sauntered onward. "Oh, yes, I do see what you mean. Not good, I must confess, though if the truth be known, I had a hunch…"

"You're not alone on that point," said Standish, "but so be it, Father. We're where we need to be."

"You recognize these characters, Father?" asked Clive.

"Yes," acknowledged the priest, "as do you, if you'd only probe deep enough into you subconscious reservoir. They're the ones Michael and I tangled with."

Clive murmured his understanding, while Stark and Sutton cursed under their breaths, assuming the cult's presence would result in an unsavory confrontation.

"We must stay strong," Father Bruno encouraged them. "We must invest our faith in the Lord."

"Amen," Standish offered, but try as she may, she couldn't shake her trepidation or her concern for Mansford. She still felt his presence—felt it so strong and near—but if so, why was she unable to pinpoint his location?

"Should we step out?" Charlie asked.

"I suppose so," said Poindexter. "It would look odd if we just sat here, wouldn't you say, Father?"

"It's not so much what it'll look like, Percival," said the priest. "We've no choice but to plunge in." He patted Standish's hand. "It's the only way we'll help Michael and for that matter, ourselves." He made the sign of the cross, slipped his fingers between hers, reached over and opened the door. "All right, folks, remember now—keep the faith."

Stark and Sutton grumbled; Clive pulled out a hanky, patted his brow to wipe away a profuse layer of sweat, each member sliding outward and stretching, their eyes peeled. Charlie, meanwhile, muttered a makeshift prayer, exiting only when the mayor conjured enough spirit to squirm from the passenger's side.

As they stepped away from the limo, the strange flock seemed to move all the quicker, the collective faces pasty, more like a group of pre-programmed automatons than those of clear heads, their shadows cast: smooth at the outset, but weird and tendril-like at the ends.

Father Bruno's two aggressors were visible at the flow's forefront, sauntering side-by-side. They turned slightly, catching sight of him and for a moment held their ground, letting others shamble around them.

The shorter's eyes widened and he pointed. "Well, what do yah know?" he cackled. "If it ain't our priestly pal."

"Yeah," said the taller, "and he's got folks with him." He focused on Standish and sneered. "Say, now, she's a dish." He winked. "How yah doin', doll?"

His stare unsettled her, and she stepped behind Father Bruno and peeked over his shoulder, feared this man, despising him, without really knowing why.

"Don't let him trouble you, my dear," Father Bruno instructed. "Block him from your mind. Block them both."

After a moment, the men shrugged and re-entered the flow from the rear, readapting their languid gaits.

Poindexter strolled over and said, "For sure, these people aren't from around here. I know the residents of Brink Town, not all by name, but certainly by face." He twisted his tie and added, "Yes, sir, beyond a doubt, these folks are foreign."

"Of course, they're foreign," Sutton growled. "All eccentrics are, when you get down to it. The weirdness rolls off them like damn water. Hell, it was even spillin' off those two goons." He turned to Stark. "And how about that stench? You smell it, don't you? It just rose from the backdrop, carried by the wind, I guess."

"Good God, yes," said Stark, glancing at Clive. "How about you, Carl?"

"Sure," he said. "Quite distinct...not quite as strong as a Guaner stench, I'd say, more muted, but offensive all the same." He looked at Father Bruno. "Keep the faith, eh?"

The father nodded forcefully.

"It all seems purposeful enough to me," said Charlie. "It might prompt us to pull a little mind-over-matter, if you think about it. Really, that's the only way to thwart any such thing. I once read this science-fiction story where the hero was being stabbed like a Thanksgiving turkey by these Martian-types, and in order for him to suppress the pain—"

"That's enough, Charlie," the mayor ordered, noticing a few heads had turned in the crowd. "Nonetheless, I believe we all know what's at hand. It's more than just pretending. It's a matter of shielding our minds...our hearts... from any beguiling influence."

"That's how Mike would do it," said Sutton. "He'd block the bastards right out, or if push came to shove, force their ugliness right back at them."

Father Bruno noticed a number of the crowd pausing in the field, gasping in nervous awe. "Something's caught their eye."

"Perhaps, it's what we've been expecting," commented Standish, her tone dry and mesmerized, "a new world forming…opening."

"New world?" Clive exclaimed. "How could that be?" He studied the purplish mist as it rolled and bounced before the crowd. "Okay, yes, I see what you mean, Miss Standish." He ambled past her and the priest, pulling a small pad and pencil from his shirt pocket. "Well, whatever it is, new world or not, it's surely newsworthy. I mean, in its own right, how rare, indeed, is purple fog?"

"Extraordinarily rare," replied Stark, sliding toward him, "and why does everything look so hazy outside the farther trees, like some damn unearthly fringe? See it?" He pointed. "Weird…real weird."

The gasps recurred and grew louder, as the henchmen pushed forward to regain the lead.

"It's happening," the taller one cried, "really happening."

"A miracle," chimed the shorter, "just like Good said…just as Tarr promised."

Within the field, the grass wavered and darkened, as additional blades sprouted and pushed outward, devouring the initial tier. In an instant, purple stained the rest of the sky, and in the cloudy stretch, there came translucent hints of arms, some small, some brawny.

"What in God's name?" asked the mayor, turning to Father Bruno, but the priest was too transfixed to respond.

"They're rather small, rather faint," said Stark, "but still there, all right… like imprints of some sort…and greenish, wouldn't you say?"

"Most definitely," Standish concured. She stood on her toes, craned her neck and then cried, "Look—look—toward the center. Something's fallen into the field."

It wasn't just one, there were many bodies falling, but not of the green variation. These were human, and they landed with astonishing grace, as if guided by some celestial hand: two distinguished-looking men, along with a striking, high-heeled woman; and then came another.

She recognized Mansford's Edwardian coat, the graceful way he landed, smooth and suave, his dagger poised and his face as bright as a summer moon…

• • •

"What is this?" the Persona asked, looking from right to left, his intuition piquing. "An inner dimension…expanding, perhaps?" He scanned the surroundings. "We've been transported and then deposited within it, and it's quickly cloaking the existing foundation." He looked at the nearest contraption, the one his mortal counterpart had inspected, the device's aura pulsating, its hollow voice whirring. "An admirable feat, if not for the evident consequences."

He noticed Good curled on the ground and nudged him with his boot. "Wake up, Herr Good. I said, wake up."

Good frowned like a confused infant and began to crawl away.

The Persona reached down, intending to slip his blade under the German's belt to yank him back, when a wistful murmur beckoned from behind.

Without turning, the Persona saw Montorto rise, her tongue gliding over her bottom lip, her fingers reaching, threatening to embrace him.

"You'd be wise to halt, Miss Montorto," he said, spinning around, his pale face catching the sun. "I do the touching...and only when I sense someone's apt to do wrong."

He raised a hand, and her posture slumped.

"Sorry to hurt your feelings," he continued, as his inner sight rippled across the transforming expanse, absorbing as much as it could, "but there's no chance of us being conjoined, particularly in a realm this artificial." His white lips adapted a pretentious smile. "Nonetheless, perhaps you can give some insight as to our whereabouts.'

She mustered her strength, crossed her arms and glowered at him. "If you're that grand an entity, you figure it out."

The Persona laughed, the sound rich and resounding, his thoughts extending, tapping her mind. He also swung several mental tendrils toward Good, Aaronheim and Tarr, inspiring them to stand, their eyes glistening with cognition.

Tarr shook his head. "Say, what gives? If you're poking about my head, I'd appreciate an immediate exit."

Even if he wished to, the Persona could not pull back, for beneath the perimeter of Tarr's consciousness, a gusher of grand allusions ebbed and flowed, charged by thoughts of growing, green specimens and accompanied by random chords of "Deep Purple". Indeed, it was the foundation for a new existence, helmed by a new church, for which the professor was guide and saint—no, make that, its flawed god.

Aaronheim knew all this too well, but his disdain was no longer designated to just the professor. Its rawness spread a hundredfold.

"*Why?*" he asked Aaronheim, forcing a telepathic link. "*Why the rage? You're part of this plan, have been for quite some time, and yet there's no doubt you despise it with all your heart.*"

Aaronheim trembled and fought the Persona's draw, and yet somehow the words flowed from his head.

"*I thought it a viable alternative, a chance to escape a dictatorial rise. My people are its sacrificial lambs, and as this vile new order grows stronger in my homeland, the world will have no choice but to bend to it. More and more of us will die, unless...*"

Montorto screamed, not from fear or physical pain, but from pure, uninhibited angst. In jealousy, she demanded the Persona's undivided attention, begged him to be his sole focus and concern.

"*Look at me...look at me...look at me,*" she shrieked, but despite her consuming fervor, Tarr's manifestations interfered.

A small arm, clutching a tiny sword, sprung up from the grass, then another and another. Beyond the farthest trees, bigger ones sprung, bearing bigger weapons, their guttural snorts cutting through the Persona's consciousness, and with the exception of Aaronheim, the folks around him straddled their thoughts and clasped their heads, grimacing and tumbling.

Tarr writhed in pain. Montorto found a moment of compassion and threw her thoughts at him, hoping to ease his anguish.

In response, the Persona gave her a mental nudge, a quiet surge, while guiding them all downward.

"God in Heaven," Aaronheim gasped, "what...what are you doing?"

"What needs to be done," said the Persona, circling the trio, lifting them off the grass. "They must know who's in control, who dictates the terms. It's the only way we can maintain control."

"*We must form a link,*" Montorto begged the men, "*strengthen it with combined focus. Trust me on this. This is my specialty...the thing I do best.*"

"I...I am trying, my dear," Tarr seethed. "I'm...I'm trying as hard as I can... but...but the specter's power...it's...it's suffocating."

Aggravated, the Persona silenced Tarr, clogging his throat to a soft gurgle. He was set to administer a similar, preemptive strike against Montorto and Good, when a curious presence drew his attention: the SIIS sect charging beyond the violet veil.

He wondered how they had achieved such infiltration and wished to intervene, but then another group several yards down, far smaller in number but also far more familiar, caught his eye. Glory be—his friends!

Father Bruno waved and from his side, Standish sprinted, shouting, "Michael...Michael...it's me... It's me."

The Persona raised a welcoming hand.

Stark, Sutton and Murphy also stepped into view, their gestures edgy and urgent, the purple plumes curling off them.

The machines buzzed and groaned. The trees pulsated, flashed, as did the sky: The sun blinked and ebbed as if perplexed, resigning its dominance.

"Ha," Tarr scoffed. "It's finally closing us in, Persona—an alternate world solidifying around us."

The Persona saw another wave of tiny men shuffling in the grass and heard beyond the trembling trees, the thud of bigger bodies approaching.

"Stand back," he shouted, causing Standish to stop in her tracks. "Stand back—danger's coming."

He swung around, his dagger aimed, his scarf flapping, his face rippling, turning bumpy and green.

Everything then seemed to slow. The Persona closed his outer eyes so that his inner ones might better expand.

A horn sounded. Steel clanged.

It was time to fight and if need be, kill.

XIII

A long, belligerent bellow sprung forth.

The Persona spotted the ogre leader, bruised and frowning, but now waving his soldiers onward, their beady eyes brimming with wild rage.

"Welcome back, old friend," the Persona said, his face resuming a smooth, ethereal white. "So, you hold a grudge? That's lovely. Too bad your ignorance outshines the reason why."

Somehow, the creature seemed to understand and leapt up, charging fast and hard, snorting as might an oversized sword swinging in all directions.

Aaronheim ambled toward Standish, Good and Montorto, while Tarr stood in pompous stance, shameless of his humiliation, rubbing his hands and blaring through his hoarseness, "Come on. Come here. Come to daddy."

Sontar bolted toward him, his minions rustling from out the grass, their weapons poised.

"And so we fight again," chirped the little king, peering into the distance. "How fortuitous." He pointed his sword in the Persona's direction. "And again, we have our leverage."

As the Persona accessed the onrush, something struck him as odd, perhaps because of its repetitive nature. Not only were the leader and followers charging, but behind them, another row of the exact same: mirror images, for all intents and purposes, with the same, damn ogre out front, a few yards behind which another led, and then yet another and so on.

"What in the world?" the Persona muttered.

"Kkkiiilll," the forefront leader growled, his counterparts declaring the same contemptuous declaration, their recycled auras so fierce that they drenched the Persona's pores as he glided forward.

One after the other, the Persona drew in each leader's scowl, absorbed the slobbering fanged-exposed fury of all those surrounding. He scrunched and compressed each hideous speck within and onto his outer face, so that it became a beacon of marauding madness and in a mighty flash, spit it all back.

An explosion of light cascaded across the field, or was it many such fields? The Persona sensed Sontar and his army hunkering from behind, replicating themselves in rapid procession, just as their aggressors had.

The Persona triggered a hard wind that knocked the ogres down like bowling pins. He then swung the raw power of his mind, and with heavy but necessary heart, pounded upon the beasts with their own brute force.

The forefront leader yelped, blood gushing from his mouth. He fell to his knees, as did his mirror images, one-by-one, and into those surrounding, the Persona plowed, his dagger slashing their arteries, severing their limbs.

The monsters' weapons fell onto the reddening grass. Their handless arms poked up in vain, their heads rolling onto the ground, gasping in the final throes of imitated life.

"Oh, my," Aaronheim cried, though more relieved than repelled. "How merciless. How vicious."

Father Bruno crept toward the ensuing carnage, while Standish continued to trip and crawl along the melee's outskirts, too rattled to keep her balance, let alone concentrate.

Tarr continued across the field, worn but resilient, kicking through his little men, chanting, "Yes, Persona—yes, yes, yes. Do the bastards in."

Inspired by the professor's exclamation, Good slipped behind him, stomping and chanting, "Purge them, Persona. Yes, purge them one and all."

Their fulsome cries echoed throughout the Persona's head, drilling deeper into his consciousness until only a cacophony of shrill laughter quelled it.

His slowed and glided across the grass, as the little creatures rose: one row bouncing up after the other, all giggling, the forefront Sontar raising a victorious fist, then his nearest imprint, and then another and another, until the original screamed in mad, reverberating victory, "Hip, Hip, Hooray. The Persona has once again saved the day."

Cheers inundated the air, but the Persona was unimpressed, his attention reaching beyond the jubilant runts, onto the SIIS members, whose shadowy shapes reached in the direction of the black-smocked scientists, who knelt at the mutilated ogres, curious but too timid to touch.

Clive waved Sutton and Stark nearer, keeping an inconspicuous distance from the sect, though remaining within earshot. The Persona, however, had no trouble hearing, fancying himself in Surrogate's vein, looking on and absorbing what transpired. Alas, if only he possessed further insight...

"It's nothing but endless field," the shorter henchman commented. "Miss Montorto's home—it's gone...or at least it's blocked by some blurry haze."

"Seems we're on the same track of ground," said the taller, "or maybe, it's been copied. Heck, that's got to be it. It's been copied, duplicated, just like those crazy creatures."

How astute, thought the Persona, but he knew there was more to the men's assessment and to determine the outcome, he continued to listen.

"We're enclosed," Clive conjectured to Stark, who in turn told Sutton, "It's like a mirror maze," which prompted the latter to add, "Yeah, a damn funhouse attraction gone totally out of whack."

Murphy then jumped in. "Whatever it is, it's solidifying. I mean, I sense it. You must sense it, too, and if it's solidifying, then sure as hell we'll end up stuck." He cupped his gun and trembled. "I'm sure of it. There's no two ways about it."

"Sweet Jesus," Father Murphy uttered, his breath strained, "have pity on us. Oh, this is bad, very bad, indeed, but again, we must stay strong. At all costs, we...we must keep our faith in you, dear Lord."

Unfortunately, the father's words failed to comfort, leaving Standish, in particular, most disgruntled. She marched past the priest, stepping toward the little men, who leapt from side to side to grant her passage.

She approached the Persona and, with steely determination, revealed what she believed he knew: "We're not enclosed...not really." She focused on his pale, gold-specked countenance, evading the sight of his blood-splattered dagger. "This occurrence—whatever it is—is, in fact, spreading...burrowing within the world we know... devouring it, as it were." She discharged a tear, but maintained a tough guise. "That's the gist of it, isn't it, Michael? For the moment, it appears we're jammed in a growing world within a larger one, accompanied by who knows how many connecting imitations."

"No matter the size or scope," Tarr corrected her, "or the carnage that's ensued, a better world it is, and I might add, one spawned from the annals of my mind...my justified mind. At last, the process is sticking, maturing in form. So what if it disregards the outer world? What once was, isn't worth saving, young lady. There's never been glory in pain, mayhem or war. In what takes root, those things will be no more."

She approached the Persona with steely determination…

"Do tell," said Standish, cocking her thumb toward the mutilated remnants. "The evidence seems to go contrary, and if it's happened once..."

"It depends on your perception," said Tarr with an assured grin. "One might say the harshness was a necessary evil, a precursor to peace. Those brutes must be viewed as germs: an infection now extinguished. From this point, paradise may very well commence, and we have our exalted hero, the great, mystical Persona, to thank for it." He gave the specter a flamboyant bow. "Yes, Brink Town's blessed savior has become ours as well."

"No," said Standish, stiffening with aversion as she regarded the specter. "Tell him, Michael. Tell him what happened wasn't what you wanted...that it's not the way it was meant to be."

Sadness overcame the man within the celestial glow and before he was aware, tears fell behind his glimmering guise. In apparent response, the machines hissed and clunked to a halt. An ominous wind whisked overhead. The purple clouds turned white; the sky blue.

"They'd have bludgeoned you, Stacey," he said, Mansford's voice permeating, "killed every last one of you if I hadn't struck the soulless things down." He threw up his hands, though the gesture looked both mortal and arrogant. "There's little more to say."

Standish's lips twitched, but no rebuttal came.

"It's quite clear," Sontar agreed. "You had no alternative. The task is complete, and now we must rejoice. We are free...free to rule...free to live as we so choose."

The replicated Sontars then leapt and cheered, their subjects following with collective squeals that soon seemed morbid in light of the brutes' blood.

Sutton shook his head and, with a sway of his shoe, knocked a few creatures away. He then gestured at the dead eyeing the Persona and asked, "This has got to be the most repugnant scene I've ever seen. What gives? Heck, maybe it was a necessary evil, but I definitely want to get as far away from it as I can. I don't know how long we're going to be here, but there's already a strange smell about the air, and to worsen it, those bodies are going to rot, especially in this heat and humidity. They'll stink to high Heaven...or the depths of Hell, as the case may be. Too bad we don't have some shovels. We could bury the damn things. I mean, what are we gonna use otherwise, our hands?" "Perhaps a few branches," suggested Good with marked cheer. "We can start with a few grooves and little by little..."

The Persona raised his hand. "We needn't act so hastily," he explained, his voice even smaller and humbler. "I assure you, one way or the other, I'll devise a plan."

"I'll hear no such thing," cried Sontar, followed by a counterpart who implored, "You've done enough Great One. Please let us tend to this. Let us repay the favor," to which a third offered, "We have the resources, and they were our adversaries, after all. The aftermath is ours to face."

Other Sontars concurred, the voices overlapping one another, and in the midst of their vocal ripples, the mask fell into Mansford's hand, gliding off his glove, then re-entering his holster; his dagger followed: all so fast, so clean that the transactions went unnoticed by most.

"Please, let us help," several background subjects now sounded uniformly, jutting their swords in solidarity. "We'll do good by you, Michael Mansford. Yes, oh, yes, we'll get the job done. Please, please, let us help... Let us help... Let us help..."

Tarr wiped a sentimental tear and regarded Mansford's flushed face.

"You see," Tarr squawked as might a proud parent, "my minions are willing to assist." He placed his hand over his heart, enchanted by the leaping, squawking members. "How touching."

"Gott im Himmel," Aaronheim griped, fishing his pockets for a cigarette. When he found none, he spat and grumbled, "Ah, please, give me a damn break."

The creatures chattered among themselves for a moment, then swung toward the severed limbs, poking and prodding them with their trite utensils, but as to what they intended to do was yet unclear. Surely, digging graves would have proven too austere.

The sect, meanwhile, led by the henchmen, flowed inward, their attention fixed on Tarr for direction.

"Come, now, my dear people," said the professor. "I say to you one and all, what we've witnessed is nothing short of a miracle...a miracle you've helped forge." He pointed at the carcasses and the little men who pranced atop them. "Now begins a new age...a new dream...a new religion—yes, a religion of our own personal and ingenious design."

Inspired, the trumpeter pushed between the henchmen and placed his instrument to his lips. The members watched him, gathering side-by-side, waiting for "Deep Purple" initial chords and when he finally he commenced, they expressed their appreciative awe.

Montorto crept behind Mansford. "You see?" she whispered. "If we play our cards right, we'll have a haven, a place to prosper, away from all our external troubles...a beautiful place, filled with fellowship, wonder...love."

The other band members joined the trumpeter, inspiring the flock to croon the lyrics of their adopted hymn.

The sweeping vocalization unsettled Mansford, prompting him to step from his temptress, as Standish slid forth.

"Who's this, Michael?" she asked, recalling Montorto's projected image, her jealousy brimming.

"Really, Stacey," Mansford grumbling under his breath, desperate to avoid a spat, "I do believe we've bigger fish to fry."

"Ah, yes," Montorto replied, eyeing the blonde, "you're Stacey Standish. So pleased to meet you." She sneered as she offered her hand. "I'm Melody Montorto." Her fingers wiggled mockingly, prompting Standish to keep her arms at her side. "It appears my letter did the trick." She retracted her hand and shot Mansford an adoring glance. "I can certainly say I got what I wanted." She licked her bottom lip and caressed Mansford's shoulder. "Oh, Michael, you've rivaled my wildest expectations. You're even grander than I perceived... so powerful...so...so dreamy."

Standish swatted Montorto's wrist.

"The nerve," Montorto seethed, rubbing her wrist. "I was only showing a little gratitude."

"I know what you were doing, sister," Standish huffed, "and I'm not allowing it." She turned to Mansford. "Michael, what's going on? I'm trying to focus, trying to understand, but nothing's clear, but this...this woman seems intent on interfering." She then regarded the prancing, prodding specimens, which with great glee proceeded to slice the mutilated flesh. "Whatever it is, it isn't right."

"Let it go, my dear." Tarr scolded. "The old rules don't apply here, not for mortals, anyway...but then, not for clairvoyants, either, nor those of ethereal design. We're one big, happy family and content for it."

Tarr's smugness irritated Mansford, making him snap, "Speak for yourself, Doctor Tarr. Contrary to what you think, I'm not on your side."

He reached for Standish and led her away, as Sutton and Stark approached from the rear.

"Say," said Sutton, looking most unsettled, "maybe it's best we just let these little cretins do their thing and keep a safe distance."

Clive, scribbling into a pad, scooted over, followed by Murphy, Charlie and the mayor close by. Father Bruno then moved toward Standish's side, glanced over at Mansford and smiled.

"Okay, we'll wander off," Mansford agreed, "find a spot to clear our heads. Maybe the rest of you can help me crack this predicament. We're in this together, after all, united by fate." He winked at Father Bruno. "And faith."

"Hear, hear," said Murphy, again patting his pistol. "Whatever comes our way, we'll deal with it, all right."

"Absolutely, Officer Murphy," said Charlie. "Danger's lurkin'. Who knows when it might strike? Those things were as big as rhinos, and you know what a rhino can do. Let me tell you, if you didn't intervene, Mister Mansford, we'd have been turned to mince-meat. Yep, wouldn't have been a pretty sight at all, but let's sure hope that's the last of them. You know, I once read in this exotic cultural magazine where—"

"Please, Charlie," Poindexter yapped, "will you keep the National Geographic lecture for another time? We need to pull ourselves together here, figure out what to do."

"You're dead right on that," Sutton asserted.

Father Bruno cleared his throat. "A little prayer wouldn't hurt, also," he suggested.

"With all due respects, Father," Clive sighed, stabbing the air with his pencil, "I'd beg to differ. We've got ourselves stuck in really some strange sector here: I'd say a kind of bubbled bunker, for a lack of a better term. I've scanned all directions, and it seems we're bordered by the same patterns all around. Maybe it's all a trick, something that registers exclusively in our minds, but there's no real way to tell. To go in any direction would prove fruitless, I suspect, at least if we anticipate escape. Of course, there's also the question of what we do in the interim…graze on the grass? Faith may calm us, prayer may pass the time, but ultimately, we're in one helluva jam." He looked at Mansford. "It's all on you, Mike. You've got to fix it. I don't know how, but it's gotta be done and fast."

"Now, now," said Poindexter, "that's all well and fine, Carl, but keep in mind that Michael—uh, the Persona, that is—hasn't let us down yet. We've all tapped into varying degrees of his special attributes. I suppose the same goes, more or less, for the other folks gathered here: that is, they're also in tune with some higher, metaphysical source. Anyway, it's obvious to me that we're all chosen, for whatever odd reason, as participants in some bizarre play, and once we know our particular roles, perhaps then we can figure the means to end this thing. Michael…the Persona…will guide us accordingly, of course, and…"

The song ended, and the congregation then turned, its collective ears geared toward the continuing exchange, their shadows stretching, anxious to absorb the words.

Tarr, in particular, found the conjecturing most intriguing, suckling every word, his lips puckered with prodigious intent. His pensive stance washed over Good and then Montorto, who had since stepped away, while Aaronheim edged in Mansford's direction.

Mansford caught the doctor's eye, and though the Persona lay dormant, a spark of his alter-ego's contagious glow flowed enough to spur the older man's resolve.

"So, what are we waiting for?" Aaronheim asked, once he was close enough. "I dare say, we may be confined, but there's still plenty of space to wander." He waved his hand behind him. "I agree with what that one gentleman said. Let that vile, green vermin do what it wants: out of sight, out of mind, though I suspect in little time, what transpires won't be pretty."

Before Mansford could ask Aaronheim to elaborate, Tarr clapped his hands, recapturing the sect's attention: "All right, people, it's time we enter the next phase." He raised his arms, gesturing his followers to follow him onward. "Come, come. No need to delay."

Good and Montorto were the first to comply, with the henchmen leading the remainder, the band mates rounding the rear.

Mansford waited for the mass to pass, taking his time to assess the situation. The others, meanwhile, took note of Aaronheim's stiffening stance.

"You don't like those folks, do you?" Clive asked, twirling his pencil.

"They're fools," Aaronheim grunted, "and you know it, too, or else you'd have joined them."

It was then that the Sontars began to cluster and giggle, their multiple minions dancing and wiggling: for all intents and purposes, inebriated.

"Those little bastards give me the creeps," Aaronheim continued. "Let's get away from them now, while we have the chance."

He shuffled off, glancing back at Mansford, who still appeared apt to watch and wait, but then stepped onward.

"Well, it's as good as any time, I suppose," said Poindexter, tugging Charlie's sleeve. "We might as well get moving."

"Wise choice," said Charlie. "I've never been much for morbid aftermaths, on the highway or otherwise. Most people are drawn to that sort of thing, want to wait it out and study the gruesomeness, but I say, for psychological stability, you gotta look the other way..."

Charlie jabbered on as they lined the field's cusp: Father Bruno moving between Mansford and Standish, the latter fighting back her tears and gazing at her man. Though he sensed her gaze, he did not flinch, immersed in his thoughts and ashamed he could not yet fix the matter at hand. Nonetheless, when she grazed his hand, he broke from his trance and then clasped hers, with tightness and conviction...

XIV

"I trust you'll fill in the necessary gaps," Mansford mentioned to Aaronheim, as he and Standish followed the scientist farther into the outskirts. "Even a few basic hows and whys might make a world of difference."

Aaronheim laughed, but the grave texture of his throat soon made him wince.

"It would be far easier," he confessed, "if the Persona were just to pluck the info from my mind, though from what I can gather, that's not the way it's done. The mighty specter comes…and goes. Now, talk about perplexing."

"True, my alter-ego surfaces sporadically," Mansford explained. "He seems to do so, though, when needed most, influenced by whatever the surrounding variables might be. Otherwise, I get my information the traditional way."

"So be it," said Aaronheim with finality. "At any rate, you're correct. I have answers—loads of them, in fact—and all for questions you needn't even ask." He tapped his temple. "Unlike the slumbering Persona, I know the answers you want."

Standish relished the jab, but gave one of her own. "I'm insightful, too, Doctor Aaronheim: insightful enough to know that you don't like those men— Good and Tarr, that is—and if I'm reading you right, you're not crazy about Miss Montorto, either." She pouted, unintentionally accentuating her Harlow guise. "Why the distrust? You obviously aligned yourself with them at one point."

"You're reading my disappointment as dislike," Aaronheim corrected her. "Tarr isn't a bad man, not inherently, anyway. Too often, he acts on impulse, visits the wrong venues, picks the wrong people to help, but no, he's not a bad man, nor is his intent."

"Do tell," said Mansford. "And yet there's still that Third Reich connection, as I recall."

"Yes," Aaronheim acknowledged, "but it exists only because Herr Hitler relishes the occult. Tarr's reputation precedes him. Der Fuhrer selects only those he believes can benefit his mad crusades. Tarr is part of that line-up, but only by chance. The professor has acted within reason: a respectable two-face, you might say. Many people in Germany have no choice but to act that way now, if only to avert persecution. I can't fault them. Tarr is no exception."

"In what way precisely has he let you down?" Mansford pressed. "I'm assuming it has to do with the experiments."

"Yes, their results to be exact," said Aaronheim. "The professor was to forge an alternative realm, one tucked beneath—or more precisely, inside—what we conveniently call reality. An ambitious but practical idea, really. Why not enter an alternate residence than be subjected to totalitarianism? Tarr gathered various Guaner texts, studied them inside-out and concluded the demons' teleportation was achieved through accentuated brainwaves, much like those of his own. He also determined that if the right frequency could be generated, if the vibrations were sharp enough, he could achieve not only the same results, but exceed them, and he did. He knew from his days as a youth that he could conjure plasmatic anomalies, shape them to his liking. With a technological push, even more miraculous things could emerge, but there were inadvertent consequences. The pompous fool refused to see them as such, mistook them for miracles and though he'd deny the fact, he certainly perceived himself a god."

"Blasphemous," Father Bruno denounced. "No man should perceive himself as such. Trust me. No good ever comes of it."

Aaronheim nodded. "Of course sir, but try telling that to someone whose dreams have taken sustenance beyond his very mind. Tarr was clearly more psychically tuned than others of his kind, and when the pigments rose from the palate of his innermost thoughts and adopted form, he saw no turning back." The scientist's expression turned grim, regretful. "The purple clouds appeared—a royal color for a royal thinker—and as for the green, well, I assume it represents the pigment of envy, and I might add, the more dominant hue for the sake of its emotional impact. You see, as much as Tarr is respected in certain, arcane circles, he's been dismissed a quack in others. Despite the disdain, he's pressed on, always experimenting, always daring to perfect his craft. He worked hard and succeeded, of course, eventually projecting three-dimensional outlines onto the very air—plasmatic, gossamer molds, if you will—projected straight from his head. Through such, he learned he could create an assembly line of cerebral copies and offspring to incubate inside their crevasses. With whatever molecules he could grab, he formed their clothing, their weapons and even influenced their behavior: all based on his subconscious yearnings, which was his first mistake, though truly all of us are to blame for promoting the process. We each took turns encouraging him at one point or another, myself included."

For a moment, they hushed, contemplating the fantastic ramifications. Perhaps, it was not so far fetched to call this man a god, but Mansford wouldn't accept that. Even the most spectacular, mental stunts would not designate one a god: a demon maybe, but not a god.

"Those larger creatures," Mansford commented, as Standish squeezed his hand, her nervousness most evident, "they obviously stemmed from Tarr's mind, as well."

"Precisely," said Aaronheim. "They've all stemmed from the same insidious source, but the larger ones initially eluded him, fizzling out before maturing or landing well beyond his immediate view, but greater numbers eventually surfaced with each new attempt. Sadly, even when Tarr knew they'd threaten the smaller offshoots, he dared not stop. The brutes could be controlled or if need be, eliminated, he said, but he needed a better, larger playing ground to test his theory: a place ripe with the necessary vibrations, where he assumed the confines could be altered to his liking." Aaronheim cleared his throat, fought back a cough. "That's when fate dictated his dear disciple, Melody Montorto, contact him. She was unaware of his ambition and reported what had manifested in her backyard. He realized what he had been dealt and sent his people to set up shop in quaint Brink Town, those who'd document and film what materialized and then send such to him, while he finished up business in the Fatherland. When the time was right, he'd fly over, maybe take up residence here, but required another component to make it all click." Aaronheim shot Mansford a hard look. "He needed a force as great, perhaps greater, than his own or Miss Montorto's: a force that could exceed what even his combined followers and advanced machinery could generate."

"He needed Michael," Standish said.

"Or more precisely, the Persona," Mansford added, "and now look at us, entangled in the heart of a madman's misguided web. What a fool I've been. Why didn't I see it sooner? Hell…why didn't the Persona?"

"It's all right, Michael," Father Bruno assured him. "All things happen for a reason. If we found our way into this, we can find our way out. It's merely a matter of how you'll get us to that point."

A knot formed in Mansford's stomach. He shook Standish's hand loose and said, "That might be easier said than done, my friend." He then looked at Aaronheim. "For all intents and purposes, we're on virgin ground. Nothing quite like this has happened before, or am I wrong?"

"Certainly nothing of this vast scope," Aaronheim substantiated. "What came before was fleeting at best, confined to meager warehouses and courtyards. The results would linger a spell, but then dissipate, the corners burning like flame to fire: yet another hope for solidification trounced."

"So then," said Mansford, "my presence helped make what now surrounds us. To be honest, I can't say precisely how I perpetuated it. Such will surely make reversing the process all the harder."

"Unless you have some help," said Aaronheim. "Sure, Tarr would not embrace such a plan, but Miss Montorto…ah, she could be persuaded."

"Now, let's not be so hasty," said Father Bruno.

"I, for one," Standish stated, "agree with the father. That woman's not to be trusted."

"True," said Aaronheim, "but she does posses extraordinary skill. It may not match the Persona's, but if combined with his, it could grant us the leverage we need." He stepped closer to Mansford and whispered, "The professor does fancy Miss Montorto, and though she respects him, her inclination is far from amorous. She has other aspirations, as I'm sure you've inferred."

Mansford looked into the distance, to where the sultry brunette stood, her back to him, but her head cocked in his direction, her eyes glistening.

He watched Tarr move toward her. He then turned to Mansford and offered a devilish nod: perhaps a way to say he knew what was developing and was up for the challenge.

"Great," said Mansford. "That's all I need: more competition."

"What's that, Michael?" Standish asked.

"Uh, nothing," he muttered "except that...well, I think Doctor Aaronheim is right. It's probably wise to play along." He donned a crooked smile. "Really, dear, it may be our only chance, and I promise, there won't be an iota of monkey business—not even close. I just need this woman to think she has a chance, if only based on our similarities, and then..."

Standish burst into tears and flung herself into Father Bruno's arms. As her muffled sobs rose, the priest looked at Mansford pleadingly, but there was no turning back.

"Do what you must," said Aaronheim. "It could be our only chance."

He waited a moment, and as soon as Tarr sauntered away, Mansford headed her way, injecting confidence in his swagger, lust in his smirk...

$$\bullet \ \bullet \ \bullet$$

"Why the change of heart?" the vixen asked, though appeared most pleased. "Was it a spat with your girlfriend, or is it simply because you want to know what makes me tick?"

"Does it matter?" asked Mansford. "Either way, I'd think you'd be pleased."

"You know me too well," she replied. "That's not surprising. We are rather like two proverbial peas in a pod, especially under these heightened circumstances." She looked about. "So, how do you find the layout?"

"Confining."

"Really," Montorto remarked, "even with all the superfluous repetition? It's really hard to tell just how far it extends, but I imagine it goes on for miles and miles: hardly confining, I'd say."

Mansford scanned the distance, the disquieting, flat plainness of it all, but more so, he sensed the rustling of its people, rubbing of their elbows, scratching their heads, the way they looked away from the huddle of cackling, little, green men and eyed Tarr and Good, even Aaronheim from afar, all for answers, wondering if this outcome was what they wanted.

"It's not the repetition that's unnerving," Mansford explained, "but rather the limited perspective it invokes." He pointed at the bustling folks. "There's a reason for their uncertainty. For all the effort they poured into this venture, after investing so much undying faith, they should be leaping for joy, and yet…"

She studied the crowd and shrugged. "I only know how I feel." She looked at him, her eyes ablaze. "It isn't a bad feeling, Mister Mansford. In fact, it's far from that." She heaved her bosom and sized him up. "And at this vantage… your take?"

Mansford paused, rubbed his jaw and teased, "It's okay, I suppose, but in all honesty, we could do better, much better, I'd say, Melody."

"Don't be silly. Our situation occurred for good reason." She glanced at Aaronheim, who shuffled among the trees, pretending not to see them. "The noble scientist may no longer have his heart in this, but he was as instrumental as anyone in getting this project off the ground. His people are endangered, you know, facing annihilation, and if the Reich's influence continues, their genocide is inevitable. Don't you see? This world within a world is a viable alternative, or at least the better option to what stands. We should hope that this world within a world continues to grow. It—and further duplications— can act as ideal sanctuaries for the persecuted…in fact, anyone in need."

"What would that prove?" Mansford asked, as politely as he could. "At best and most, we'd have more people enter the folds, though they wouldn't all be good, or they could turn bad down the line. It's just the way life goes. Hiding from one's problems, regardless of how cataclysmic, isn't the answer. It's only a temporary fix."

"You might be right," she said. "Still, I'd rather see this through. If we were to combine our mental resources, we might positively impact what's been forged. Sure, your girlfriend won't be pleased, but she's not suited for this kind of venture. None of Brink Town's citizenry is. They may dream, remember snippets of strange things here and there, but that doesn't make them part of a special ilk. I'm not saying we're god-like, for heaven's sake, but at the same time, I think you can conclude accordingly."

"God-like," Mansford emphasized, trying to maintain a calm demeanor.

"Something akin to it, anyway. We're far from normal, especially you. If a man can transform his physical structure so drastically, alter his very constitution in the wink of an eye, I'd say he's at the very least god-like. Wouldn't you?"

Mansford winced and was about to redirect the conversation, when a burst of screams, male and female, pierced the air. He saw the taller henchmen pointing and hollering as others moved around him. "Look—look what the little bastards are doing."

The shorter henchman squeezed alongside his friend, gawked for a moment, then cupped his mouth.

With Montorto at his heels and Tarr joining the sprint, Mansford bolted toward the gathering, pushing his way through until he could see what they saw.

Several Sontars leapt among the carcasses, slicing thick, green tiers of flesh with their blades, tossing the slithers to their minions, who accepted such with grateful grunts, lapping, chewing, gulping.

"Most peculiar," said Tarr with tremulous regard and then stretched his arms, as if in some vain attempt to wipe the vision away, but he froze, only his fingers twitching like spindly leaves of branches against the wind. "I'd never have suspected…"

Montorto stared at the horrific sight in numbed awe, before finding the strength to look away, her eyes falling on Mansford's stony countenance, hoping he might offer some rationale for the grisly display.

"It's…it's not possible," Tarr blabbered, forcing himself from his stupor. "Such bestiality wouldn't be in their nature." His fingers fell limp, and his arms dropped to his sides. "They come from me…my mind…and this…this is clearly not me."

Good marched over to him. "Perhaps you should be more forgiving, Professor. They're like children. You've told us this. They obviously don't know any better. They must be taught…groomed in basic etiquette." He patted Tarr's shoulder. "It's all right. They're at least disposing the remains. That's all we wanted. Let's turn round, not look back. Let them finish the task."

"It's the devil's work," Father Bruno spewed with a repelled stretch of his lips.

"It certainly is not," Tarr chastised him, thumping his chest. "It is my work… miraculous work…only like any preliminary version, a tinge flawed." He looked again at the nauseating feast, and to add fuel to the ghastly fire, the Sontars acknowledged him with little waves, blood dripping from their fingers and bearded chins. "Indeed, there must be a logical explanation for this, some little thing I may have overlooked."

Mansford leaned toward him. "Your plan is devouring itself, Tarr. That seems the gist of it. It wasn't meant for implementation. By its underlying nature, it might never be."

"Nonsense," Tarr chided. "This…this is but a minor setback, I tell you. I…I can remedy it…redo it."

Anxious murmurs sprung from the crowd. People pointed upward, prompting Clive to leap among them, scribbling fast, while his eyes rose to the sky.

"It's going weird again," he said, "deep purple, but turning kind of orange, too, and look at the sun…the moon—both poking through at the same time, but on opposite ends, like big, melting orbs. Really, Mike, it's gone too far. This just isn't right."

Mansford agreed, but as much as he wished to decipher it, he was at a loss.

"What do you want us to do?" Murphy asked him. "Just say the word, Mike."

"Maybe build a shelter?" suggested Stark, seeing no harm in a little practicality. "It'll keep us from harm's way, if the sky should…well, if it should… you know."

"Shelter, my foot," Sutton berated. "What good's that gonna do? If we're gonna get hit, Buster Brown, we're gonna get hit, whether from above or below. We're vulnerable, no matter how you slice it."

Poindexter bounced over, Charlie at his side.

"I say we block all this out," the mayor offered, "with our minds, through our concentration. After all, we've done it before, more or less. I'm sure we can do it again. Yes, we gather together, get our heads together, focus hard and as Father Bruno says, invest a little faith and pray. That ought to make it go away." He gave Father Bruno a hardy thumbs-up. "Think about it. If our collective conscious put us here, maybe it can get us out." He looked to Mansford for support. "Isn't that right, Mike? Don't you agree?"

Mansford nodded, and though he had no clear plan of action, he mustered as much mettle as he could and wasted no time to mimic Poindexter's robust tone. "You're right, Percy. That's the thing to do." He turned, absorbing Aaronheim's face, then Father Bruno's, Standish's, and then beamed his own into the crowd. "We focus, and that means all of us, SIIS included. We figure this thing out together as a group, elbow-to-elbow, mind-to-mind."

The words, though spoken via instinctual rote, comforted the tense participants and let even Good and Tarr to step calmly into their rallying mass.

Montorto chose to linger behind, staring at Standish, who remained at Mansford's side. Oh, how the sight repelled her even more than the creatures' vile feast.

Now more than ever, she acknowledged the need to eliminate the competition. It was the only way to ensure her consummation with Mansford… the Persona….and nothing—especially some love-sick, bubble-headed blonde—was going to deprive her of that.

"This just isn't right."

XV

"**M**aybe," Clive speculated, "it's one of those deals where it's got to get worse before it gets better." He scrutinized Mansford's cold expression. "Maybe, given time, the boundaries will fall, fade away through natural means. The creatures can feast all they want, but there's only so long they can sustain themselves. They're probably not even designed to multiply—all males, right?--and as for the sky, heck, maybe it'll smooth itself out, turn nice and blue again. Before we know it, we could end up right back where we started, like nothing happened."

"Or," said Stark with a cynical pout, "this thing goes on long enough for those little things to turn on us, or maybe, just maybe, the sky will just, you know, explode. I mean, I'm no chemist, but its texture looks mighty gaseous. Yeah, whatever's up there could even trickle down and suffocate us all."

The garrulous speculation unnerved Mansford. There he was, his closest friends breathing down his neck with every conjecture in the book, while he remained impotent, the Persona as good as dead.

Tarr looked on the verge of tears, and though Good tried to placate him with a few encouraging whispers, the attempt only irritated the professor.

Even the mayor looked flustered, beads of sweat rolling off his brow, with Father Bruno equally on edge; though at least bold enough to do his job.

"Let's focus," the priest requested with unsteady cheer, spreading his arms outward, not unlike in a sermon. "Let's form a mental bond, see where it takes us. Often, the simple act of prayer, the mere means of expressing one's faith, can work miracles. Don't be afraid. Try it. You'll see."

Grateful for the priest's initiative, Mansford offered Standish and Father Bruno each a hand and clasped hard and tight.

In the process, he noticed Montorto's face, gazing past those who now formed the makeshift circle. Maybe, he thought, he had reached her, given her the incentive to deconstruct Tarr's wayward results.

She then smiled at him and with her penchant for poetry, conveyed, "*Yes, indeed, we'll unite all right...show them how it's done...save and savor this day and then you and I will be as one...happy and free.*"

No, that's not what he wanted, not while he grasped Standish's soft, warm flesh. Sure, he could play the suave charmer, but he could not lie or deceive. Did Montorto not understand that? Could she not read the truth beaming from out him?

He broke his stare and shifted his eyes to the now languid Tarr. He sensed the professor's harbored resentment, his desperate need to sustain his glory. Mansford then looked to Good and read the impetuous zeal behind the man's obedience and was reminded how each of us wore our own mask. How could any of us ever hope to conjoin on any effort, when such intense, personal convictions brewed beneath?

His hand slipped from the priest and then from Standish. He grew light-headed and in his humility, fancied himself floating, but it was only his mind, his spirit, that rose at this point.

Above, the orange and purple streaks crossed and blended, under which a sense of day and night passed, all too fast. The little creatures continued to giggle and gnaw without pause. Then, without warning, smoky brown fissures broke from the brush, between the trees, as the fields continued to multiply, one added onto the other, as far as the psychic eye could see.

Again, Montorto's curvaceous frame entered his head, the scent of her perfume, and though he fought the lure, he still fancied the idea of her removing her clothes, one sensual strip at a time, the people around her sliding back, constricted by their own shadows, until their presence, though strong, no longer mattered.

More fissures broke, their brown plumes puffing upward like Indian signals, to which Aaronheim bellowed, "Oh, no—it's happening again. Why... why won't it stop?"

Mansford's inebriating fantasy died. He stumbled backward, Father Bruno catching him from behind, as Standish grabbed his hand, patting it to ensure he stayed vigil. People raced passed them, a number weeping, panting, cursing in an overlap of English and German.

Mansford took a deep breath and focused with all his might, absorbing the burning, jagged crevasses that had become superimposed throughout the immediate field, while the resulting, smoldering residue thickened the air.

Aaronheim, now roaming the inner outskirts, waved at Mansford and pointed down to a wide indentation expanding at the base of the farthest machine. With extra vigor, the machine shook, buzzed and hummed.

"You see," he cried over the dinging clamor, "this is the sort of thing that happens: smoky portals rise before all else fades. Maybe this particular device is sustaining the fissure...perhaps vice-versa." He leaned down. "Yes, just as I feared, the hovering hole is taking root...expanding." He looked up at the violent sky. "I dare say, every single speck of it is."

"Of course," said Tarr, strutting into the dissipating circle. "Why would it be otherwise? The phenomenon may be plagued by some kinks, but those will iron out. You must give the process time to meet fruition, you fool. Even the devices know this, or else they'd not have reactivated. The vibrations will strengthen what surrounds us. Soon, all will be as intended. That's more than the sound of wishful thinking, more than a prayer sprung form some hollow theology. This is scientific deduction, culled from progressive, cause-and-effect, and I promise you, the range of its effects will not be denied."

The machine clattered louder, and its counterparts answered with equal gusto, creating a ricocheting whirr about the perimeter, which then echoed in and out the adjoining fields.

Mansford joined Aaronheim near the hazy hole, but when they peered inside they saw only spiraling smoke, their faces struck by immense heat.

"Alas," Aaronheim lamented, "things are too far gone now." He looked at Mansford in woeful desperation. "So, what does your intuition say? Are matters truly as doomed as they appear?"

"I'm not sure," said Mansford, again trying to rekindle his inner power. "I do sense solidification, though, but at the same time, we may be experiencing some uncanny form of tectonics here. The same thing is happening above: one force fighting the other for dominance." He studied the machine with intense fervor, hoping to absorb as much of it as possible. "I believe the vibrations triggered the devices back on, and in turn, they've begun forging a different atmosphere, one unnatural to this earth." His expression tightened, as his brain screamed and cranked with forced enlightenment. "The variables imply something disastrous is about to strike…a quake, perhaps…and not just from the ground."

"You're wrong," said Tarr. "The conditions will allow me to manipulate the elements to our advantage. This is precisely what I desired, what's necessary for us to survive."

"Heed the professor's words," Good chimed. "He's an expert on this sort of thing. The present results may be more dynamic than what's come before, but the conditions are the similar. Yes, they can be controlled, just as he says."

"That's what troubles me," said Mansford, "this matter of control. There's far too much of you in this, Tarr, from the good to the bad, and from my vantage, the latter is clearly overriding the former. The more you try to force this to your liking, the worse off it'll get. That won't settle well for any of us."

"Nonsense," Tarr blared, throwing up his arms and stomping back to the machine.

"Never be quick to judge what you don't understand," Good scolded. "This man created something from nothing, plucked it right from the undercurrent of reality, right from out the limitless stretch of his imagination. Nothing like it has ever come before. He knows its particulars. Only he can fix it…if it does, in fact, need fixing."

"Oh, it needs fixing all right," said Mansford. "The professor's planted all the wrong seeds, and unless we find the means…"

"Means?" Good guffawed. "Your impact on this has been minimal at best. What good has the Persona been? Where's the great entity now?" He walked away. "At this point, you've no right to intervene, Mister Mansford. If you do, you'll only impede us, and the same goes for your friends. You should have kept them out of this from the start."

"Ah, let him go," Aaronheim growled. "There's no reasoning with his sort. They can bend the facts all they want, but the great professor has fumbled. He twisted the variables of teleportation into duplication and at what cost? Oh, I should have foreseen the risk in such long ago, stopped it when I had the chance."

Out of nowhere, a long, smoky plume reached Mansford's crown and circled it. He waved it away, but was curious from where it had come and again peered into the hole, and this time caught the deep, fiery glow within. He trembled.

"What's wrong?" asked Aaronheim.

He did not answer, being too intent in extending his vision. He then looked up, past the device, into the next field, at the same machines, surrounding the same trees and brush.

He looked at the sky above this duplication: clearer than it was above, its contrasting pigments in evident infancy. He noticed a few stars poking through, twinkling between the blurry sun and moon. He watched one orb, and then another, take turns becoming more distinct, stretching, writhing, implying an urge to explode, or maybe even implode.

Suddenly, a trace of smoke—grayish white and too small for the others to discern—trickled between the formations, falling into the purple haze. He recognized the form and smiled.

"Excuse me," Mansford said, pointing yonder. "Must head out."

Standish edged toward him, tears still streaming, her arms open wide, but he raised his hand, halting her, as Montorto watched.

"*Whatever it is you need to do,*" the temptress conveyed, "*I'll be there. Please… let me go with you. Let me help.*"

Her plea was strong, but for the moment, Mansford dismissed it, refocusing on Standish's trusting stare.

"I won't let you down," he said and blew her a kiss.

He then sprinted into the mist, beyond the blood-splotched core…

XVI

"**S**urrogate," he cried. "Where are you? There's no time to waste. I need your help—desperately."

From out the hazy center, like a stretching plant, the saint rose in his green robe and gingerly stepped over what Mansford now recognized as little, sprouting arms, their still forming fingers reaching upward.

"As you can see," Mansford said, pointing at the formations, "this venture has proven a most confounding one."

Surrogate's smoky mask faded. "I'm well aware of the urgency, Michael, or else I wouldn't have made my presence known."

"I appreciate it, but of course, if only you had—"

"Let's bypass the complaining, Michael," Surrogate chastised with a dismissive swipe of his hand. "For what it's worth, my arrival was swift. Besides, in this particular scheme of things, your perception of time is skewed: a wicked side effect of the dimensional unfurling. There are other unstable features involved, as well, with more developing, I fear. The question now begs: what to do?"

"The Guaner influence tipped it," Mansford charged. "I say, we focus on that. If Tarr hadn't looked to those damn texts for inspiration, none of this may have occurred."

"A valid point," said Surrogate, stepping over another patch of mushrooming limbs. "Man should never fiddle with what he does not understand, and the emergence of this dimension is one grand case in point." He looked up. "Precarious imitations are spreading." He pointed down. "It's all quite half-baked, though, but all the more dangerous as such. Things will grow ever more petulant before any particular state seizes dominance. Whether above or below, one portion will devour the other."

Mansford sniffed a vile vapor, and it reminded him of a time not long ago. He glanced to the side and saw one of the machines, near which a floating fissure smoldered. He walked over, rubbed his nose and then positioned his face close to the cauldron-like haze and beheld its craggy slope.

"That's it, old sport," Surrogate encouraged, gliding to his side, "always be intrepid. I remember how bold you were that night in the cemetery, how you assumed your role so well after springing from my cavern…"

Mansford recalled the moment in vivid detail, which in turn, intensified his perception, magnifying what lied inside: just as he feared, a black, eight-limbed beast, its hide rising as it slept against a ruddy slate, its four beady eyes open but glazed, its snores like the croaking of some monstrous frog.

"It's a leader," Mansford stated. "It's evident by its size, its musculature: maybe not as regal as the Great Beguiler, but from the looks of it, as strong and most likely, as vicious."

Surrogate tugged Mansford back. "I fear there are many more just like it, itching to spring. They only need the required nudge: a rattle, a shake, and they're bound to awake."

"Then it's set," Mansford said. "I certainly can't stop what's progressing."

Surrogate shrugged. "Perhaps." He glanced beyond the farthest trees. "It doesn't help, either, that others are assisting that progression along."

Mansford followed Surrogate's gaze and saw Tarr enter the adjacent field's fringe, poised between two towering trees, Good at one side and Montorto at the other, her fetching form still enticing him.

Mansford closed his eyes and prayed, "I have to stop it, somehow, someway."

"I know, Michael," Surrogate said. "I wish I could do more to help you see it through. I've offered all I can and can only suggest, the prime villain isn't always the most obvious one. You should know that better than anyone. Often, you have to go through others to find the actual emanation of evil, but when you do, it's only then that things will fall into proper place. Yes, it all comes down to a matter of identification. Please consider that."

An ineffable ripple then swept across the field, flattening the fledgling arms and grass. The distasteful stench increased.

Mansford eyed Tarr, studying his stiff, determined pose, the way he widened arms and fanned his fingers, this time with confidence.

"He'd like to conjure a few more ogres, or orcs...or whatever those beastly things are supposed to be," Surrogate remarked. "Ironic, considering they'd only attack his wee favorites, but no matter. People do desperate things under duress. Poor fool...if only he knew what lurks below. Such holds more danger than anything he could conjure from scratch. At least you know what makes those particular beasts tick, Michael. You fought them—and won."

"The Persona won," Mansford corrected him, "but what's it matter if he's dormant. I wish I could conjure him. It's as if the dimension is preventing me from doing so."

"The Persona resides within your instincts," Surrogate explained, "in your impulses, or as Father Bruno might say, in your faith. That's where you'll find him, Michael...in your faith. Despite what you may think, it isn't that hard to conjure."

Though Surrogate's words proved inspiring, Mansford's heart was weighed by uncertainty. He tried to shake it, but when it prevailed, he panicked. He looked back at Tarr, Good and Montorto, wanting to thrash them, or at the very least, rub their faces in the ill-conceived views. Yes, that's what the Persona would do, if only he were there. He would make them taste their own medicine.

It was then that, in this lamenting rise of righteous zeal, Mansford's feet lifted several inches off the ground. His scarf snapped against the air. His dagger slipped into his glove, and his mask snapped onto his face. However, despite this physical change, he could only hover, not soar. Confused, he glanced back at Surrogate, but the saint had flown, leaving the quasi-deity's gaze to peer through the mist, upon the feasting creatures.

Among the carcasses, he noticed more smoking holes, a few along the ground, others hovering a few feet above, wavering about as if to gain a better station. He laughed at the absurdity of it. Why would things be otherwise in such a surreal realm?

He noticed Tarr staring at him from the opposite end, Montorto and Good still standing alongside. He felt the trio's distrust flowing in tune with the ground's disquieting vibrations.

With no recourse, he glided toward the professor, seething in a way that suited Mansford more than his spiritual self: "You've no idea what you're doing, Tarr."

Tarr's brow wrinkled, his contemptuous current prevailing, and to worsen matters, Montorto abetted him with full, conniving force, her focus wrought with vengeance and vindictiveness.

The Persona picked up pace, his jacket snapping like a sail as he traveled, but just as he began to land, he churned an intense gust that made the professor topple, stumbling into Montorto and Good, who crashed to the ground with him.

Enraged, Tarr sprung up, yelling, "It was a mistake to have recruited you. You've…you've no idea what you're doing and now…now you're tainting the process with your recklessness. I don't know what Miss Montorto ever saw in you…why…why I ever thought you could help."

"You're the one who's tainting," Mansford countered, gesturing at the hole-ridden field. "Look at what you've done. You think you're manipulating the variables, twisting things to suit your needs, but you're only disrupting what lies below—waking it up, provoking its numbers."

"What are you talking about?" Tarr growled, as Good helped Montorto to her feet. "They're just fields, duplicated to meet my plans. So what if there are a few flaws. Why can't you see the potential I've laid before you, the veritable blessing it is?"

"It's a curse, Tarr," the Persona countered, lips stretching like melting putty. "There are Guaners within those fissures. Their positions have already been juggled…misplaced. It won't take long before they realize something's wrong. They'll want to know what's skewed the status quo."

"Come now," said Tarr with a half-hearted chuckle. "That's impossible… improbable. It's—"

A deep croak thundered from below and echoed among the fissures. The little men stop chewing, their eyes shifting in fear.

The SIIS members looked to one another, quivering and whispering.

"What was that?" Montorto asked.

"Your worst nightmare," Mansford answered.

Another reverberating croak followed, then another.

Tarr tugged at his lip, curled a strand of his hair. "Oh, dear Lord, how many? Tell me—how many?"

"Your guess is as good as mine," he answered, "but from the look at those crevasses, I'd say there's at least a couple dozen at this point, and in the event you skipped it during your research, some of these beasts tend to be large, even more so than your inflated ogres. In fact, the one I saw was exceptionally massive—a leader of its kind—and if the others are of the same ilk, and I suspect they are…well, perhaps the less said the better. Nonetheless, the ogres' blood, combined with the machine's persistent vibrations, guarantees trouble, and be assured, these monsters will attack anything that stands in their way."

Simultaneous roars then burst, obstreperous enough to shake the ground.

Gasps rose among the SIIS flock, the henchmen taking the initiative to lead the members toward the outskirts, but what good would that do?

"What gives, boss?" the shorter asked Good, spotting him in the slow flow.

"Yeah, tell us," demanded the taller. "This stuff wasn't in the plan when you hired us."

"No need to get bent out of shape," Good quipped. "I promise you, Professor Tarr will keep the situation under control. He'll mend it, reverse it. You must give him time."

"Bull," cried the taller, his nostrils flaring. "We're through with this professor clown and his lies." He raised his fists and shook them. "Come on, folks. Let's make these high-brow soothsayers do their job and get us the hell out of here. If they won't, we'll slap them damn silly until they do."

The SIIS screamed its collective consent and then in one immense swoosh, charged, but through spontaneous desperation, Mansford had honed his defenses, clapped his hands and hurled them back—not hard, but with enough thrust to make them pause.

"Damn it," the smaller henchmen moaned, trying to maintain his balance. "The odds never roll in our favor."

The Persona, elated by his surge, wasted no time to hover before them and declare, "The odds are stacked against us…all of us…if we act irrationally. We'll dig ourselves into a deeper hole if we're not careful. We have to stay clear, able…and indeed, faithful. It's the only way we'll survive."

Mansford's friends moved nearer: Father Bruno and Standish toward the center, both beaming of pride. Tarr, Good and Montorto, meanwhile, had realigned, huddled and tense, but thankful for the Persona's save.

"Wise words," said the Father, pausing before his friend, absorbing his conviction and turned to the crowd, so that they might also taste the intensification. "We're with you all the way, Persona. We sense your power… sense your belief."

"Yes," said Poindexter, "we believe." He scanned those gathered and smiled. "Help us reinforce our bond. Let's bring this predicament down."

Mansford savored their vehemence and gazed deeper into the farther field, at the creatures rising and leaping. He then eyed those closer, who had resumed their deplorable feasting, and then the holes, inhaling their nauseating stench while suckling the ground's mounting vibrations.

Yes, the Guaners would rise. It was only a matter of time. He was ready, but realized the demons must make the first move. He was strong, but not yet equipped with the gamut of his strength to yank each from its own dimensional portal. That would take too long, prove too distracting. Some would slip by and gain the upper hand. It was imperative, therefore, that the beasts emerge of their own insidious will and as simultaneously as possible…

XVII

B eneath a curled cloud of crimson, the Persona sat with his fingers locked, his legs crossed, the humming of the machines predominant.

The adjoining skies overlapped and streaked: one harried hue splashing onto the other, smearing the unearthly duplications of suns and moons.

Tarr studied the specter. Good stayed at the professor's side, egging the professor on with quick, urgent whispers: "If I were you, I'd take over the scene. You are, after all the creator, Herr Professor. This dubious mystic…he was only along for the ride a would-be accomplice to the cause."

"Listen to him," Montorto whispered. "It's obvious he can't be trusted. "I know. I've tried to reason with him, even offered myself to him, and for what? You must make a move, my dear Raimond. Deep down, your people want you to rise to the occasion. Regardless of what happened earlier, they'll stand by your side."

Tarr remained sullen, steadying his stare, roaming within a myriad of exasperating thoughts.

Then much to Montorto's dismay, Standish tiptoed toward the Persona and placed a consoling hand upon his shoulder. He acknowledged this with a subtle nod, but like Tarr, remained entranced.

"It's all right," Standish told him, following his stare into the field's heart, where insinuations of Sontars and their minions shuffled about. "Do as you see fit. We'll wait. We'll wait as long as you need us to."

"As long as you need?" Montorto squealed for all to hear. "How sweetly naive. You'd be wise to hush, my dear, unless you wish to make a fool of yourself."

Standish bristled at the vixen's audacity. "And maybe you should mind your own business," she countered, folding her arms and glaring. "In case you haven't gotten the hint, he doesn't want you. Yes, I know it stings, but that's the way the cookie crumbles."

"What's going to crumble," Montorto hissed, stomping toward her, "is your head after I pound it in." She raised her fist. "You're way out of your league here, you…you scrawny, little harlot."

Standish fanned her nails. "Harlot? The only harlot I see here is you."

Their primal surge lured the Persona from his trance, but before he could intervene, the gals had already latched onto each other, scratching and clawing.

In response, the guttural croaks resumed. The ground rumbled again. The holes wavered, swirled and spread. Perhaps, thought the Persona, the anticipated moment had arrived.

"Please, now," Father Bruno begged, forcing himself between the women, "this ungodly behavior won't solve a thing."

The Persona smiled to himself, for he knew that contrary to what his friend claimed, their brawling was, in fact, becoming a necessity draw, filling the air with abundant tension and lust, attracting bands of smirking Sontars and their eager troops across the corresponding fields, to snicker and point their swords at the salacious melee.

The women knocked Father Bruno out of the way, hitting the ground, their fingers intertwined in each other's hair. The Persona, meanwhile, heard the Guaners snorting within their niches, whiffing the women's sweet scent, listening, contemplating.

Good lunged past Father Bruno, eager to intervene in the fight, but as he reached down, the women slipped from his grasp, rolling onward, squirming past beyond Mansford, toward the creatures that flowed from various points throughout the grass.

Murphy stepped in, waving his hands to ward the specimens back, but when a thick flood of them swung from the left, it was Stark and Sutton who hurried in, kicking them away.

"There's more comin' from the rear," Charlie shouted, shivering at the creepy sight. "Gosh, this batch looks pretty plumb. Man, do they ever smell like raw meat." He stumbled back as they quickened, their weapons angled at him. "Get away from me, you horrid, little, green-fleshed fiends. Get away."

Standish tore the top of Montorto's dress, and with great gusto, Montorto reciprocated, their shoes flying off as they twisted and groaned, Good and Father Bruno again in pursuit.

The women's harried panting distracted the creatures, who abandoned Charlie, and in a beeline move, eschewed Murphy, Stark and Sutton, circling to face an arrival of their boney reflections, all participants hoping to gain a better view of the sultry match. In a matter of seconds, they surrounded the ladies in a makeshift ring, their raspy voices phasing from English to German and back again, some whistling, winking and blowing kisses between their spirited yelps.

The Persona's heart raced. His body felt light but firm.

At the machine-base fissure, he saw four clawed fingers reach upward, stretch outward, racking the upper soil. Another set of claws then broke against the dirt, expanding the opening, granting room for the beast's four-eyed head.

"Sweet Jesus," Father Bruno whispered, stepping way from the ladies to watch the eight-limbed thing rise like a giant shadow and breathed its hideous stench. "Foul…so horribly foul." he gagged and wiped the sweat from his brow, then with quivering hand, crossed himself. "I never thought to see its likes again, unless in a nightmare, and even then, I'd not have suspected it to look this monstrous, this evil."

Good then stumbled away from the entangled women, watching as more towering Guaners surfaced. "It—it can't be," he gasped. "They look exactly like in the old texts—four arms, four legs and those eyes—those terrible, hateful eyes."

The women bounced off each other, distracted by the mounting smell. They then glanced at the flanking row of Sontars—both plump and thin—their soldiers leering behind them.

"Don't stop, fair ladies," Sontar, the First implored, blood-smeared and bloated. "We wish to see more," he cackled, then smacked his lips, "lots more before we have our way."

"Your way?" Montorto jeered in repulsion, pulling a loose slither of fabric across her breast. "I don't think so, buster."

"Never mind those little ones," Good said. "Look at what's coming now." He turned to Tarr, who remained wide-eyed and despondent. "Snap out of it, Professor. What do you plan to do?"

Tarr steadied his gaze on Mansford, who began to hover with arms outstretched, his ethereal sheen spreading.

"I'll talk to him," Tarr murmured. "I'll reason with him."

"Reason?" said Good. "About what? This is your world, your problem. Only you can fix it."

Tarr shoved his subordinate out of the way, and to the specter said, "You can't do this alone. You need help—my help."

Standish crawled from behind them and when close enough, grabbed Mansford's leg and begged, "Don't listen to him, Michael. It's a trick."

"Stay out of this," Tarr hissed, looking again to the Persona. "Just like you, I've studied Guaner lore. I know their strengths, their peculiar abilities. Truly, I can help."

"But I fought them," Mansford replied, his voice deepening. "You haven't. You couldn't possibly know…"

"Yes…yes, of course, I could," Tarr stammered. "I've understood ever since Miss Montorto conveyed it to me in her letter. I understood the details she shared about Brink Town's collective reverie, all those mad dreams, all those damned vibrations. There's no doubt I can help you achieve your goal all the faster. I know what to do. I've already planned it, you see."

The Persona verified Tarr's sincerity. Somehow, someway, the poor, tormented soul cared, but there was still so much danger in his impulses.

"Please, Michael," Standish begged, "don't take the bait. There's too much at stake. You know how ferocious these beasts can be. The last thing you need is someone to throw things off track."

The Persona considered her words. She had good cause to be cautious, not only in Tarr's regard, but for the pending Guaner uprising. The Great Beguiler had taken her parents, turned them against her. The damned thing had even managed to warp her mind for a time, turning her into its living puppet.

Tarr stepped in front of her. "You'll helm the fight," he assured Mansford. "You can peer inside my head if you don't trust my intent. Please, I beg of you. Do it before it's too late."

Several Sontars bolted toward Standish, some pricking her ankles with their swords, others bouncing upward, their bellies ramming against her thighs. In disgust, she released Mansford's leg and began swatting the creatures away.

Murphy came to her aid, the officer's pistol aimed at another approaching flow. In response, the little monsters shrieked and jutted their weapons,

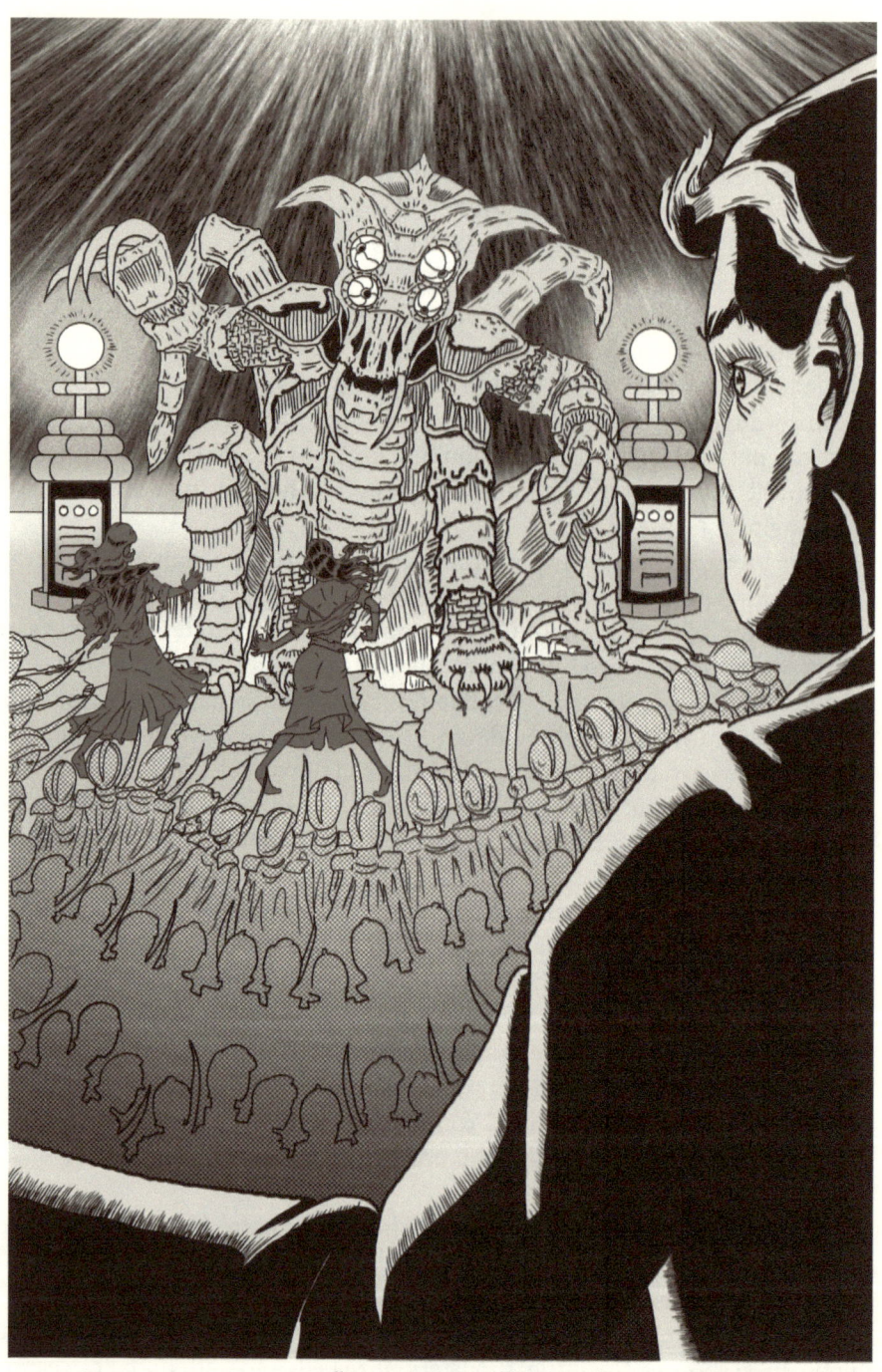

"It-it can't be..."

determined to seize the woman. All the while, the Guaners progressed, their eyes steadfast, their limbs cranking with weird fluidity.

"Time is of the essence, Mister Mansford," Tarr continued to reason. "Absorb their hungry eyes. Toss their hatred back at them, if you must, but I can help you…help you adapt a size and shape to rival their own." He stretched his fingers, threatening to pull the specter down, but caught himself. His countenance softened. "I have a blueprint in my brain," he promised. "I had hoped to use against the Reich if only the circumstances, the right moment, had come, but that idea—that golden nugget of a thought—still thrives within me. It can be hatched now, Persona. It only needs my blessing to live and breathe, and with your accompaniment, there's no telling what we can achieve."

The Persona was intrigued and ascended a few notches higher, but as he looked down, he peered into Tarr's skull and saw the embittered man's harbored dream: a large, dark chamber with transparent girders comprising cage-like structure, walls that rolled inward with massive, mold indentations vast and wide. It had been imagined with meticulous care and would have entered reality if only given the chance, but that made it no less impressive or practical.

Upon closer scrutiny, its indentations contained compartments, or rather glassy outlines, configured to hold four, muscular limbs and from the rough looks of it, a mammoth husk thick and ridged. Clearly, it was an intended prototype, its innermost design geared for revenge, for it had run through Tarr's thoughts a thousand times over for that inevitable moment of comeuppance.

Levers were pushed and cranked. Around the spectral design, profuse purple plumes ascended, as bright-green goo gushed from the cage's inconspicuous portals: shaped from invisible specks, summoned by the professor's hidden rage. Like lava, it poured into each translucent crevasse and with an air of dread, then cooled to an odd, organic pallor.

"*See it?*" Tarr said, elated by his reverie's progression. "*If you do, then you see as I see.*" He laughed at his own cleverness. "*And if you see as I see, then you can see through my creation's eyes.*"

His creation's eyes? What a unique thing to convey, the Persona thought, and yet, he could not deny the consciousness that rose from the thing's budding mind. It was then that he let himself feel as it felt, the iridescent flesh covering him…covering Tarr…letting it consume their combined visage.

The Persona maintained control throughout, even as the slime soaked his pores, filling his soul with emotions raw and wild, saturating his coat, scarf, gloves and dagger; with each passing second, becoming more than a mere dream, more than a mad hope.

The substance appeared to dissolve his glove and in an instant, became a bone-like extension of his hand, reinforced by a base of thickened, rounded flesh. The transformation stung, for it seemed to twist his arm straight up into his head, the pain guiding his perception.

A dark chamber became a large warehouse, not unlike the one Aaronheim helmed. Men stood inside a perched, glass-paneled compartment along its side wall. They were dressed in stylish, gray outfits, some sporting monocles like Hans, others with authoritative goatees. All looked immersed as they passed Guaner spikes among them, reflecting on the objects' consistency, acknowledging how these ancient pieces were akin to the cogs and gears that operated the vibrating contraptions, which the Persona now realized flanked the colossal cage.

A familiar man stood in the center of the compartment, his hairdo Moe Howard's, his mustache Charles Chaplin's.

The chamber then wavered, impacted by the machinery's pulsations, which burped thick, purple plumes.

"*I always played their game,*" Tarr lamented, his inner voice woeful and strained. "*I gave them misleading answers on anything that pertained to the arcane, but what did they care? They only ever wanted to peddle their propaganda. I despised their lies, their smugness, their ceaseless need to invade, to take what they never deserved.*" His tone grew terse. "*My allegiance was only ever to the SIIS...never the accursed Reich. I hated it with all passion, all my might.*"

Tarr laughed, his voice echoing without direction. They felt the creature's mouth open, its throat constrict, but it emitted no sound. The absence of sound seemed to startle the beast, which set forth a chain reaction among the translucent girders, causing them to rumble, some even to fall. Tarr and the Persona had become the mighty monster, stretching its roundish, clawed paws, making it charge like a mad ghost beyond the imaginary warehouse walls, into the purple twilight.

They blinked the monster's eyes, felt its blood coursing through their own, with the Persona steering its colossal frame, Tarr's thoughts hanging on.

The dream was now more than a dream. It had infiltrated the newborn reality within their repetitive bubble, popping as if from out the air for those entrapped to see: a heaving, tree-towering anomaly, emerging from the first field's far end, opposite the Guaners, which upon spotting it, slowed and croaked defensively.

From above, a red blemish formed and slid over the creature, following its slow but steady progression. Through the Persona's peripheral perception (a rapid, aerial pan), the creature's formidable characteristics solidified, brimming of lurid slime.

The Persona could tell its husk was covered in thick strips of organic armor: flat silver, smudged in black. Its head was rough and round, its curled nostrils flaring bull-like, its eyes pupil-less and red. A long ridge stretched down from its crown to the tip of its nose, where a long, daggered horn protruded, its origin more than evident.

The forefront Guaner paused and with several brisk scrapes, kicked the grass. Its spiked tail stiffened as it reared, and once heightened, it slapped its chest with its upper paws.

"Michael?" Standish cried, skidding toward the lumbering beast, confused by the circumstance but sparked with enough intuition to know the thing cocooned the essence of her man. However, when the creature continued to move toward its probable adversary, she turned to Tarr, who appeared at the great beast's rear, gliding by her as if tugged on a rug, his eyes closed, his arms folded across his chest. "You bastard—what did you do to him?" she screamed, infuriated by his contented stance. "Look at me, you bastard. What black magic is this?"

Father Bruno grabbed her shoulder and pulled her back.

"Whatever it is, my dear," he whispered, "I'm certain Michael agreed to it. He knows what he's doing, just like on that night he brought Ben Gyler down."

The Guaner stomped, croaked and took a few steps forward, before again rearing and pounding its chest, but all the while, the Persona kept keen focus through the eyes of his bestial disguise.

"Come, now, dear, step back," the priest told Standish, guiding her toward the flailing, little warriors, who Murphy had just corralled via a point of his pistol. Meanwhile, Stark, Sutton, Poindexter and the jabbering Charlie edged in, leaving Montorto to merge with the crowd, finding her way between Good's wary henchmen.

Good now remained beyond the main flow, his expression cold and cruel, even as Aaronheim stumbled his way.

"Each side is set to strike," the scientist predicted, trembling as he absorbed the length of the field. "I dare say, when these things clash, it's going to get downright hellish."

"Perhaps," said Good, meandering toward his colleague. "The atmosphere is certainly malleable, just like in a dream. The very air is being bent." He removed his monocle, wiped it on his sleeve, his bloodshot orb bulging with uncertainty. "You're right. There's not much we can do now, except withstand the battle."

The head Guaner bowed its dark crown and in a quaking snap, sprinted. In response, Tarr's fabrication followed suit, springing from its rear legs via the Persona's command, carting the still catatonic professor by some invisible cord.

Purplish dust churned behind the man until somewhere in the impetuous spree, he was cut loose and hurled like a rag doll into parts unknown.

With a colossal thud, the behemoths collided, the Guaner wrapping its arms around the green goliath's bumpy back, raising its furry palm to administer hard, clawed slaps and to each side of his opponent's hind, stinging stabs of its tail. However, the Guaner grew frustrated, panting and croaking in the realization that its efforts were in vain: its opponent's coarse flesh evidently impregnable.

Nonetheless, the Guaner continued to fight, exposing its incisors, wishing to bite, but as its opponent swiveled and bucked, it found at best it could only chomp at the air; and in little time, began to look small and frail in comparison to its counterpart.

The Persona then dug the thing's paws into the ground and with the finesse of a guided arm, reared its daggered horn upward, slashing the Guaner's neck. Blood gushed from the demon, which unleashed a whistled croak, its eyes wide in disbelief, as it fell backward, causing a thud so loud it made the machines totter and spark.

Like an upside down spider, the Guaner flailed its limbs, its chest rising before caving in, breathless and cold, and as if on cue, a gush of purple fog enshrouded it.

The SIIS members gasped and moaned as the creature's defunct scent wafted forth, their shadows reaching out only then to fizzle like dying flames. In panic, some danced about, in hopes their merriment might wipe the sight way, or muttered quick, nonsensical chants: spurts of makeshift, religious zeal that had no apparent impact.

The remaining Guaners whimpered and croaked, as the great, green beast shook their leader's blood from its horn.

The little men appeared delighted by the sight, darting about with careless abandon, many still clustered around Standish, gnashing their teeth and blowing her kisses, though several opted for Montorto, to whom they projected similar advances.

"Seize the moment," declared Sontar the first, raising his sword. "Seize the day. Carpe Diem. Hip, hip, hooray. Upon their sumptuous flesh, we shall feed."

As the henchmen stomped at those surrounding Montorto, Murphy fired into the air, causing a number of the wee ones to squeal and cup their ears.

"What's the deal?" squawked the taller. "Damn cop's only gonna get those little bastards more riled."

"Yeah, damn, typical cop," remarked the shorter. "Always meddlin' when there ain't no need."

"Hush, you morons," Montorto berated, her face pale and flushed. "It doesn't matter what any of us do now." She peered past Murphy, watching as the great, green beast poised itself, its head bowed, its horn poised. "Illusions can't be controlled, especially when they've progressed this far. Even if we were to realign our minds, the effort would be fruitless. Professor Tarr may forge whatever he wants, but so does the damned Persona." She suckled a sob. "If only I hadn't expended my powers on all those insipid parlor games, on a romance doomed to fail. I should have nurtured my strength Maybe, just maybe, I could have made some impact, but now it's too late…far too late…for any reprieve." Her tears rolled. "I truly fear, the worst is yet to come."

The Persona arched forward to inspect the Guaner's chest, now cracked and gurgling, revealing a smelly slither of an androgynous shape: a human form, more or less, not yet complete, one that would have been conjured to roam an earthly plane.

The repellant sight triggered memories of the Great Beguiler and his breed's penchant for deceit. The Persona knew he had to stop these vile things before they massed. What if they grew so strong in number that they gained the upper hand, unraveled the circumstance before them and then somehow found the means to break through the bubble? They did possess the innate means to teleport, and if they thought to trigger it, what then?

Another shot rang out. The goliath turned and watched Murphy fire yet again, the shot obliterating several of the skinnier minions, while several others leapt onto Standish's legs.

The Persona swayed his mountainous frame toward her, but his chivalrous intent proved a mistake, for unbeknown to him, two Guaners had circled round and pounced upon his back, snapping and clawing between his steely ridges, their stench numbing his senses.

The goliath reared, shaking with enough thrust to toss the demons from its back.

In the backdrop, he heard Standish cry, "Get them off me. Get them off. They're biting—biting," but as much as he yet wished to aid her, he realized the futility. He had no doubt his friends would rescue her. For now, his priority remained the Guaners. He had to strike them down.

The two demons sprung themselves upward, as more of their brothers crept nearer. Then one by one, they lunged atop him, but he was wise to hunker and then swung his horn upward.

His head ripped from left to right and back again. He then opened his mighty jaws and snapped upon their flesh, tearing it with merciless vigor.

The Guaners grimaced and gurgled, the first tier falling hard, leaving the next to wade in, but the green beast again cut upward. Another Guaner tier tumbled and another and another…

The Persona endured some injuries about his head and neck, but the lacerations only advanced his zeal, inspiring him to slam the demons onto their backs, allowing him to dart down into their meaty chests, slicing his horn straight up to their bullish necks.

The layering aroma reeked of sewage. Fleshy matter protruded from out their bloody chasms—a flimsy arm, a flapping hand, a malformed head—only to dissolve back within pools of their bubbling bile.

Undaunted, the Persona continued his relentless attack. Onward the Guaners lunged at him and fell. The machines hissed like kettles. The skies merged over and over again, the pigments thinning, but the fiery patch above expanded, rounding out like some watchful eye, flecked by the pigments that entered it.

The moons and suns pulsated, one overlaying the other, and the space between them appeared to tighten: one ghostly imprint invading the other, their queues aligning from both visible ends, though how far the mad procession stretched was impossible to say, for the fields had also shifted and tiered, stirring a mounting, doleful mist against a bobbing, violet haze.

Murphy fired several more shots, until his gun clicked empty. Casting shadows that were truncated and faint, the sect screamed and darted, but to where could they go?

"Stacey's bleeding," Poindexter declared. "Hurry. Hurry. It's bad."

"I'm on it," said Aaronheim, tearing a slither of his shirt sleeve. "I'll press it against the wounds. That should stop it."

Standish moaned as he proceeded, and though the Persona—or more so, the rising Mansford—wished to abandon the fight, he realized he could not turn back.

The last four Guaners charged, oblivious to their inevitable defeat, fangs gleaming, claws outspread, and the Persona, barreling forth like a mad triceratops, sliced into them with a final, wild swoop, stabbing down, turning them into putrid mush, all in one fell swoop.

The beast coughed loud and hard, but the intonation sounded human, weary and disoriented.

Screams continued to rack the Persona's head, and dead smack of the blood-drenched field, he turned upon the dampened earth and stared into the distance.

The original Sontar—identifiable by his pompous, belly-plopping prance—waved his blade, ushering his many reflections and minions onward, but Stark, Sutton and Clive kept them at bay, kicking those who dared come near, hurling them back, their bodies bruised and, in several instances, cracked.

Murphy and Father Bruno continued to flank Standish, who remained sprawled on the grass as Aaronheim tore another sleeve and dabbed.

Throughout this, the mayor rounded up Tarr's frantic followers, as Charlie paced before them, spouting a breathless spree of nonsensical assurance, much to Montorto and Good's displeasure.

In a last, desperate ditch, several of the tiny creatures shot for Murphy's feet, but he knocked them away like bowling pins. However, others moved toward Stark, one springing from behind and biting down upon his derriere. The poor man cried out, swaying his hips, so that the thing ticked much like one of his famed Clutching Hands.

Clive held Stark's wrists, as Sutton pinched the creature's legs, tugging until the thing sprung loose and flung it into its snarling imprints, where it landed upon several of their clustered blades.

The Persona scoped the quieting expanse, the fissures coming back into view, but exuding a steaming emptiness. Now victorious, there was no need to stay in bestial mode. However, as he plodded through the carnage, something most unsettling caught his eye.

It was the field beyond the next, superimposed, now littered with copies of the ogre's nibbled bones and inundation of more little men. He saw the same crevasses and holes, the advent of the Guaner's crown: rounding out and darkening, exuding the same slithering motions as the one he had defeated. As the beast squirmed its way out, more of its kind surfaced, releasing the same croaks and stench.

Aaronheim watched in awe as the Persona thudded onward, set to reengage.

"It's happening—happening all over again," the scientist whined. "It's as if their damned spirits have been transplanted." His face grew long and drawn, his balled sleeve slipping from his hand. "So, this is how it goes. The duplication never ends. If only there were a way to break the cycle…"

The Persona heard Aaronheim's plea, but what could he do? He could only tear the demons down, rip through them for as many times as they would manifest, and yet maybe—just maybe— he thought, in the midst of it all, there was still a way to gain what he wanted. He was, after all, encased in little more than a man's thoughts. Perhaps these remnants could be derailed, if he just administered enough focus, enough faith.

With several quick thuds, he cut through the trees, squeezing from out one field into another, his elephant-like soles leaving behind ominous, bloody blotches within the violet mist.

As the machines' purrs deepened, Aaronheim placed Standish into Father Bruno's arms. Murphy and Sutton inspected Stark's rear. Poindexter and

Charlie kept the mounting sect in check, except for the henchmen, who had broken from the group, leaving the disenchanted Montorto also to wander off. Oh, how she yearned to join her heart's desire, whether man, deity or beast.

Clive waddled past the vixen, scribbling his final page while trailing the goliath, but out of nowhere was hit by an abrupt gust, which slapped him onto the ground.

The odd sight piqued Montorto's interest, and though intuition begged her to stay, she nonetheless approached the journalist.

However, before she could reach him, the encircling gust rounded back and struck her as well, but she mustered enough finesse to avert much of its impact, ducking and rolling under its erratic sweep.

The Persona did not know what to make of the occurrence, but also saw no immediate danger in it. If anything, the phenomenon insinuated the onset of change, and with matters already dire, he suspected they could not get any worse…or could they?

The Persona then realized Montorto caught him overhead—and with renewed yearning, reached up to him—her brainwaves yet demanding a link, an alliance, but he ignored her plea. He still had a Guaner to face. This time, however, he took no obvious stance of attack, instead suckling the bending air, absorbing the vibrations spurred by the mirrored machines. He also felt a strange softness surface within the sector's tapestry: ripe to reshape, squeeze… destroy. Perhaps another promising sign…

He smirked, as much as his facial formation would allow, and peered into the Guaner's four, glistening eyes and pulled from out the beast's unbridled ferocity and in no more than an instance, fired it back.

The Guaner staggered backward, gagging, choking. Those behind it caught its pain and did the same, each rearing upward, grasping their necks, ticking their tails, wagging their slimy tongues in vain attempts to breathe.

Satisfied, the Persona snorted, but restrained his urge to charge. He now had the power to do something more, something faster, and imagined that his brain harbored an immense heat ray. With utmost concentration, he took a few anticipatory steps back and then showered energy—as red as blood, as hot as hate—upon the demons, forcing their molecules to separate, dissolve, and along with them, so did the fledgling, little men, in seconds reduced to green globs upon the grass.

The machines clattered and shattered, their panels melting to silvery mush, until only bright-white auras stood in their place. The auras soon doused, revealing yet another field in its wake. Like the one prior, it mirrored the ogre's severed limbs, Sontar's rising army and of course, the ever present Guaners.

...the phenomenon insinuated the onset of change...

Without hesitation, the Persona dispatched them all—entire field included—into a luminous explosion, moving on to another stretch and more hateful participants.

Montorto shivered from the incessant impact of it all, doubting she could withstand the mind-bending strain, but somehow, someway she managed. She suspected that the Persona, if only in an indirect way, guided her along, making her suffer as he suffered, savoring the Guaners' rapid disintegration, but also giving her the stamina to prevail.

She then realized, with much lament, what little emphasis the mighty entity had bestowed upon her. Somewhere through his temporary facade, his inner eye looked beyond her, through the dying fields, until he fixed back upon the trembling Standish, still cradled by the priest.

She fumed at the sight. How dare the spiteful specter rub it in her face? And yet, it was only expected: the only reason why she had written the foolish girl. Mansford—more so than the specter that dwelled within him—had more basic aspirations, of which alas, it appeared one such as herself could never be part.

Despite this and perhaps because she had no other recourse, she clung to her elusive hope and forced herself to dip into the Persona's peripheral perspective, viewing from all angles as he continued to blast the beasts. Through his manic diligence, she felt his faith, but even more so, the rise in others who watched, particularly Father Bruno, whose conviction multiplied a hundredfold within his twinkling eyes. Yes, the people now believed, and their vibrations empowered the proceedings to an extent she could have never imagined, propelling the process so fast that it clicked before her eyes like a deck of cards, pacifying her mind like a sweet gush of fine wine.

The sky flashed, though not of lightning, but rather of raw emotion. Somehow or other, through the zeal of the Persona's heart and mind, the barriers were, in fact, breaking down into weird, crooked sheets of red, dripping like blood upon their heads, the gusts continuing as the process progressed, visible by highlighting splatter: for all intents and purposes, a series of revealed puzzle-box panels pushing toward completion.

Good wiped his brow and growled, "What is this? What's happening?" He clasped his crown. "If it's not one damn thing, it's another."

More machines crackled, sparks spewing at their tops, their panels dropping...melting. Purple steam seeped from their open corridors and covered them, while curling high, consuming the crimson droplets, only then to inflate, descend and dissipate. The contraptions' cacophony continued toward an ear-puncturing pitch, but when the collective rumble threatened calamity, the devices hissed into cold, silent deaths.

"The sky," Aaronheim cried, "it's opening—opening right over the creature's head, pushing through the red. I can see it—yes, oh, yes…what a beautiful, majestic sight…and blue beyond it…oh, so alluringly blue."

To the dying patch above, the Persona aimed, grasping at the remaining red, suctioning the essence of what tiered below. The spectators swayed and stumbled through the mutilated Guaners, goo and ogre bones, all of which crumbled to dust upon the slightest graze.

Montorto, meanwhile, grew as light as a kite and floated past the bleary outskirts into a patch of purple residue, which just so happened to hold the yawning Tarr and several of his flailing offspring, who appeared most eager to leap and yelp to wake him up. However, a few of the specimens were stationed a few feet yonder, still prancing and taunting Standish and Father Bruno, with others boldly sailing between Murphy's legs, slithering onward in a serpentine queue to join their brothers who in precise emulation, approached from the other end.

"That's right," Tarr cackled, adapting a paternal slant. "Come, my dears." He widened his arms. "Come to daddy…"

The Persona's husk sagged, fizzling to a translucent outline of the thing he once was.

Wearily, he looked upward and saw beyond the hovering red, a floating, blue-robed shape with a smoky face. He sighed in relief. Hallelujah—the surrogate saint had arrived!

"*Show us what to do,*" he prayed, his humble voice puncturing his celestial confinement. "*Show us the passage out of here.*"

As he awaited a reply, his view fell upon Standish, her face contorted in pain, blood streaming down her buckling legs, ready to collapse, if not for Father Bruno's sturdy frame.

She gazed up, her eyes gleaming, and then—of all astounding things— the wind lifted her—lifted them all, in fact, though Standish remained first queued. She twirled and whirled, a smile forming on her face.

He extended his arms—yes, arms that were once more Edwardian garbed— and snapped his clean, shiny dagger back into its holster. His pale face curled a smile to match her own.

When she was close enough, he grabbed her, and with this, the blood faded from the sky and along with such, her legs; her wounds healing as well.

Others rose among them, looking uncertain, turning to one another, their shadows retracting in nervous humility, their powers either quieted or for the moment, defunct. Still some were bolder in their response, either cursing or stammering their doubt, bouncing up, only then to descend, until they came to their senses and rose again.

"Holy cow," Stark cried, grasping the startled Sutton, the two levitating fast. "This is incredible." He spotted Father Bruno, who shot by. "Isn't it, Father?"

"Indeed," Father Bruno replied with a big grin. "Now that's what I'm talking about, Ned. Faith is the answer." He chuckled. "Look how buoyant it makes one." He glanced at the many weightless bodies that continued to approach, but also noticed the henchmen still relegated to the ground, stumbling about as they gazed up, fear and doubt in their eyes and despite what transpired around them, a lack of belief. "The evidence is clear, my friend. Only through faith can one rise."

The sect locked their sights on the Persona, trying to reach him, making him their guide. Standish held onto him close and tight. Blue sky stretched before them, ever widening, ever safe, and before they knew it, what was up, then became down.

Through subtle means, they had entered a transparent tunnel, which shifted and closed. They were still in a portion of the maze, the Persona inferred, but one created for delivery.

They dipped without apparent cause and saw the field resurface, but instinct told them it was of the original design, solitary and clear, and not far from it stood Montorto's abode. Vehicles were parked by it, and far beyond that stretch, more trees, grass...homes.

"Oh, my," Standish giggled, as the Persona swept her down to the ground. Once her feet were planted, she pointed in the distance. "Am I wrong, but...but what's that over there...to the left? Do you see it?" She squinted and trembled. "There's purple around it, and I dare say, it's fairly wide."

At the farthest corner of the field, the Persona spotted the jagged portal. He extended his vision, pushing deep inside it, until a scenario, aglow in envious green, formed: Tarr surrounded by his Sontars, but they were no longer congenial, leaping about with vicious zeal, swinging their swords at him with harmful intent.

"Go on," Tarr dared them, his voice cracking with betrayal, "you ungrateful spawns. Go on. Keep trying." He hunkered and swatted a few of them, but with their simulated steel, several pricked his fingers. He licked the blood away and then stood, shaking with contempt. "You think you can hurt me? Well, I'll show you who's boss. If I made you, I can unmake you, too." Again, they jutted their swords, but this time only gnashed their teeth and licked their lips. "All right, if that's the way you want it..."

Sontar the First, pudgy and bloodied with pride, shot onto the professor's leg, jamming his blade into his thigh. Blood spurt. The professor shrieked and kicked his once favorite son high into the air...

Standish squeezed the Persona's arm and whispered, "I can see it...see it through your eyes. Dear Lord, how horrible. We have to help him, Michael. We have to—"

Without further adieu, the Persona glided toward the portal, but before he could reach it, it flashed from view, leaving a trail of meandering, pale purple, which within seconds fell victim to the wind.

The Persona paused, his scarf tightening about his neck, tucking back behind his neck. He slipped his gloves into his pockets; the mask fell, and in a wink of an eye, mortal Manford stood, bearing an agitated frown.

"I'm...I'm real sorry," he said, more mouthing the words than enunciating them, "but...but I guess there wasn't much I could do to help him. The portal was there one second and then gone the next..." He headed back toward her. "It was a fleeting anomaly, I'd say. If there were more time, perhaps I could have reached in." He shook his head in regret. "Nonetheless, I assumed he's not alone. If I'm not mistaken, Good's goons are still there, along with the creatures, of course, but on the whole, who knows how precarious matters are...how long any of it will last."

The sect, yet bedazzled beyond expectations, paid little mind to Mansford's mortal guise, let alone his pronounced speculation. At this point, they were only interested in whispering among themselves, the frazzled band members huddled off to the side and the scientists approaching their shattered machines.

In disgust, Good stepped away from them and approached Mansford, one eye calm, the other bulging against his monocle.

"Truly, Herr Good," Mansford explained, sensing the man's disdain, "I would have rescued the professor if only I could. I'm as surprised by what happened as—"

Good reached behind and pulled a shiny Luger tucked behind his pants.

"You think I care about Raimond Tarr?" he guffawed, aiming the pistol at Mansford's brow. "He was only ever a stepping stone, a high-stationed lunatic who I was forced to tolerate." Good's tone turned more Germanic, as his anger rose. "I was only acting as a clever foil, watching him devour his own mental excrement, over and over again. I never believed he'd have taken it this far, or that the fabled Persona would have gotten involved. Ah, how life is so full of surprises."

Mansford now realized that Good was the inconspicuous villain to whom Surrogate had alluded. Good had no loyalty to SIIS. He only tolerated its presence so that he could report back to his superiors, share so they might turn it against anyone who dared oppose the Reich.

Montorto raced toward her false ally, her face wrought with disbelief. "What's come over you, Hans?" She eyed the gun and cursed herself for having missed the obvious, or had she? Good was still a good man. He just had to be. "What's this going to prove, my friend? I can appreciate your pain, your disappointment, but what's done is done."

"Oh, I see," said Good, sneering at her, "you want to play the good girl now, but it's too late for that. You are the disappointment, my dear, right along with your prestigious professor—both pawns of great Persona, who used you like puppets on a string. Your psychic prowess has been proven weak."

He turned to Mansford. "My superiors will be delighted by what I've learned. As for Tarr, I never trusted him—none of the Reich did—and as for you, Mister Aspiring Immortal, you served your purpose well. Like dear Miss Montorto, you proved yourself no more than exalted, bumbler, easy to deflect and block. No matter... I will report what I've learned to the Fuhrer ...share such with Germany's most exalted psychics. They'll modify this fiasco...find the means to make it a success." He clicked his heels and with a complacent grin, cocked the gun, eager to squeeze the trigger. "Now, Herr Persona, it's time to say good—"

A shot rang out, though it did not come from Good, but rather Murphy, who nailed Good straight in the heart.

Good's monocle popped from his head. His cheeks puffed, gasping for breath and with that, fell backward, landing flat upon his back, the gun skidding to his side.

The SIIS flooded forward and murmured.

"Holy smokes," shouted Sutton, after pushing his way through. "You got him—got him real good, Jack." He leaned over the bug-eyed corpse and gave the officer a curious glance. "Say, unless I'm a bad count, I thought you used up all your shots."

"I did," Murphy confessed, "except for that extra bullet I keep in my pants pocket." He winked. "Just in case, you know."

Father Bruno also entered, the onlookers respectful of his presence, granting him easy passage. With lament, he regarded the body, pulled out his rosary and kissed it.

Poindexter then waddled forth, accompanied by the fidgety Charlie. The mayor waved his arms before the crowd, asking its members to "Stay calm. There's no need to fret. Savor the fact that we're again on solid ground."

As if in prophetic reply, what yet remained of the machines broke apart and in the distance, Montorto's abode creaked and moaned, threatening collapse.

"Whoa," said Stark, shaking his exposed rear. "What's this now?" He skipped toward Mansford. "Come on, Mike. Really, enough's enough. Whatever it is, make it stop."

"I think it's some sort of aftershock," Mansford speculated. "The landscape's settling, as well, I suspect. Trust me, Ned. It's probably best to let it pass."

"No, please," Montorto screamed, bursting from the scene. "My home…my home. We must save it. We must…"

"Come back," Mansford cried, running after her. "There's nothing you can do. It's unsafe, Melody. Come back."

Like a jackrabbit, she sprinted off her toes, shrieking wildly as the front porch swayed, the windows shattered, and dust blew from out.

"Come back, Melody," Mansford persisted.

She glanced at him and yelled, "I can't. It's all I have—all I have now in the world."

She leapt up the steps, charged through the front door, at which point, under an obstreperous snap, the façade fell inward and the roof downward with resounding impact.

Montorto's tearful, dying wails filled the air. People rushed forth. Mansford shot beyond them, into the smoky veil, but the unsettling tingling down his spine conveyed the pursuit's futility. He bowed his head and sighed.

Father Bruno caught up to him, followed by Standish. They looked at the cataclysmic layout and each placed a consoling hand upon their man, as the fleeting scent of Montorto's perfume, nearly forgotten among recent events, seemed to trail through the breeze, before fading to nothingness.

An ominous quiet followed. The air brimmed of finality, regret.

Father Bruno whispered the Lord's Prayer and to Mansford remarked, "She played with fire, Michael. She should have known the risk." He looked to the sky, so righteous and blue. "The Lord will tend to her now…as well as Herr Good…and any others…dead or alive…who've fostered this insidious plan."

"It only goes to reason," said Mansford. "There's no doubt, their fates are sealed."

Poindexter strutted over. "My goodness," he huffed and wheezed, "what a sight. You know, folks are going to question this: a house inexplicably collapses in on itself, kills a pretty girl. The inquiries will never cease. I can hear it hitting the fan right now—'Mister Mayor, Mister Mayor, what do you know? What did you see?' "

"I'll take care of it," Clive said. "The angle may be questionable…that is, a tad unethical… but it only makes sense to keep the details tight and clean. It'll appease the public, as well as the police."

"I'll go along with that," said Murphy with a reluctant shrug. "We certainly can't tell the truth on this one. Folks would assume we were lying, anyway, pulling some sort of stunt. Certainly not worth the trouble…right?"

Charlie nudged his way in. "Right you are, Officer Murphy," he exclaimed, rubbing his hands, "but take it from a man who does a lot of reading, you'd be surprised by all the otherworldly activity going on out there. Lots of people experience it, and lots would be willing to tell their tales, if not for being ridiculed. Heck, even for us gathered here, this isn't the first time we've encountered the strange, and I'm sure that goes for these other folks, all shadowy and in tune—"

"Okay, Charlie, okay," Poindexter grumbled, "we get the point. The less said, the better."

Clive looked to the priest. "This jive with you, Father?"

"Well, perhaps I really shouldn't say," Father Bruno mumbled. "Nonetheless, I must admit, this whole escapade would be hard to convey at face value, despite the spreading intuition among the area's citizenry." He rubbed his chin and grimaced. "I'd imagine the good Lord would give us a pass with a white lie or two, at least I pray that's the case."

"I'm sure it'll be fine," Mansford assured him with a wink. "I, for one, have faith in that. I believe the Persona does also."

Father Bruno smiled.

Mansford then felt a strong draw, looked into the distance and discerned a smoky-faced figure, now in casual, muted-blue shirt and pants, gliding with ironic grace several yards behind the foreboding wreckage.

"Excuse me," Mansford said. "Must attend to something. I'll be right back."

"But Michael," Standish moaned, "where are you going? The dust is too thick. Unless you're going to conjure the Persona, there's no way you'll possibly see anything out there…"

"Oh, I'll see," he replied with a joyful skip. "I'll see quite clearly, in fact…"

Surrogate paused and nodded through his smoky countenance, the plumes of which then pulled away to reveal his earnest countenance.

"So," said Mansford, slowing his gait, "you can obviously see what's happened—not a favorable way to cap off this venture. I only hope it's over."

"Yes," said the saint, "it is…more or less. Despite the enormity of its unsavory parts, you performed as well." He gestured with lament at the collapsed house, fingered a subtle blessing. "Sad that certain matters ended as they did, but as your honorable priest so noted, when one plays with fire…"

"Yeah," said Mansford, "a reasonable enough deduction, All the same…"

Saint Peter glowered at him. "I understand, Michael. I understand all too well. You wonder why there's so much turmoil in the world, why life on so many levels should be such a struggle. You wonder what your part is in it, whether it be man or spirit; why the Lord and his agents don't readily intervene." His expression softened. "The doubt...the lack of faith...makes sense when you see dictatorships rise, crime swarming the streets, when anxious people embrace makeshift religions, hollow churches and upside-down beliefs. You ask why...why all this madness? All I can say is, life is but a grand and often infuriating test. The Lord sets the standards, places the variables, and we test our characters in the interims. Where we end up is how we react. Once in a while, in the heart of all the confusion, someone like you comes along, a chosen one who chooses the right team to fight the right fight. That's why I gave you the mask. You always had that special quality, Michael. You just needed the right circumstances to receive the required blessing. Nonetheless, when bad things occur...and I assure you, son, they most certainly will continue...you'll be there to play your part, as will your proven people....and I...well, I will be watching as the Lord instructs, giving the required nod whenever it's deemed necessary or appropriate."

The saint's words struck a chord and made Mansford appreciate his unique designation, and yet he still could not help but feel dejected, embittered.

"It's just hard working in the dark," he explained, "never knowing which way to turn. It's a heck of a way to exist, and when my friends are forced to take things to the limit, only then to forget...ah, that really stings. It especially hurts seeing how it affects dear Stacey. She tries so hard to keep a clear head. The same goes for Father Bruno, who fights tooth and nail to nurture his beliefs, and then there's poor Carl, who never fails to jot it all down, but for what? Phil, Ned and Jack are in the same conundrum, meaning well, but never gaining any viable traction. What's any of it mean if their efforts are dismissed? You see, that's what troubles me. So much of the time, what we do seems in vain."

"Nonsense," Saint Peter scoffed. "Every good action resonates, and for what it's worth, your team performed most exemplary during this latest bout. This time, what transpired won't fade, and even what came before will now remain. I have His word on it, Michael." In homage to Father Bruno, he made the sign of the cross. "It's ordained."

Mansford seemed relieved. "Good, then...I've no complaints, but now with that done, what's next?"

Saint Peter grinned and pointed to Tarr's disenchanted sheep. "Those who are meant to forget will forget. They will find their own way, through whatever beliefs they so choose. That, too, is ordained."

With this, the members turned and began sauntering away, flowing into their various queues, meandering off to their vehicles...the band mates tossing their instruments into the trunks; the scientists rubbing their eyes, anxious to get home, wherever such might be...

After a time, the ground rumbled, suggesting another quake. This led the stragglers to pick up the pace and others to rev their engines, then squeal from the vicinity, but there was no real threat. The saint's serene stance confirmed that.

A faint, violet streak rolled from out Montorto's flattened home, saturating the cracked boards and snapped girders, reducing it to a bumpy mush.

As the phenomenon continued to expand, Mansford's team stepped cautiously forth, uncertain what to expect, but in the end, they simply watched the forefront extension roll beyond them, over Good's shell, leaving only the dusty impression of his Luger behind. The gaseous mass then slowed, ebbing and flowing until it formed a fine, twinkling cloud, before moving on to parts of the field.

The mystified group then heard a sizzling sound and turned to see the fog had crept onto the machines' remnants, saturating them for a moment, only then to rise, leaving fading, purple puddles in their wake.

"Will wonders never cease?" asked Mansford.

"I think not," Saint Peter chuckled. "At any rate, this little sweeping of the evidence will help tie up loose ends. Ironically, it's the final spurts of Tarr's would-be religion that's finalized the process. If anyone should ask what happened here, feel free to say whatever you wish." He folded his arms. "Indeed, by all means...feel free."

"Appreciate the blessing," said Mansford and looked into the farther distance, toward Aaronheim, who was meandering among the careening cars, fanning his arms with dismissive flair, shouting at the top of his lungs, "Go, then—go, you cowardly fools. You were only ever a bunch of cultist clowns, anyway, with all of your misguided views. Good riddance, I say."

"So, I guess that ends it," said Manford. "And yet, I still can't help but wonder, what's become of Tarr? What will become of him, Surrogate?"

He turned to his mentor, but the saint was gone, his signature trail of smoke circling upward.

"Of course," Mansford mumbled. "Will wonders never cease..."

He kicked through the rubble, meeting up with his friends, who regarded him with curious glints.

"Who was that man?" asked Standish.

"What man?" Mansford replied with unconvincing innocence.

"The one you were talking to," she said, pointing back, "the one who suddenly vanished. He was dressed rather officiously, like a businessman, I'd say."

"Business man?" Stark interrupted. "He had on baggy pants and a smoking jacket, like any old gent."

"Old gent?" scoffed Stark. "He looked pretty spry to me, and as for a smoking jacket—it was definitely a sweater."

"No, no," said Murphy, "it was too thick and tattered for that. He was a hobo, I'm certain, overall quite patched."

"Of course, he was a hobo," Poindexter concurred, "but one of distinction: a specialized variation, well worn and traveled, more like a seasoned adventurer, I'd say, kind of like Hemingway."

"He was your general groundskeeper type," Sutton corrected. "I know the look…have sported it myself…the sort of fella who puts in extra hours at work because he gets nagged by the wife a lot."

There came a long pause and then Charlie said, "Gosh, I don't know. It was hard to see through all that dust, but if I had to venture a guess, I'd say he was a hodgepodge of any man…and every man…I'd ever met."

Mansford scratched his head and turned to the one yet to comment. "Your take, padre?"

Father Bruno wrinkled his nose and after long pause, confessed, "I say Charlie's assessment is correct. He was at the heart and soul of it, your proverbial everyman, but with the well-rounded, humble make-up one might find in any errant saint."

Another pause followed, capped by knowing glances. There was nothing more to say. They knew they had been blessed, now bestowed with the means to remember, just as the saint had said.

"That's right," Aaronheim yelled, as the final car zoomed from sight. "Find a nice rock to crawl under. That's where your kind belong…"

The scientist sensed the somber eyes upon him. "Oh…uh, sorry." He cleared his throat. "Letting go of my pent-up frustration. Should never have agreed to that insipid scheme. It was destined to fly south." He headed over to them. "Only wish I could compensate for what happened."

"It's not your fault," said Mansford. "You meant well and learned a good lesson as a result. When you play God, you're bound to fall short, or as Tarr discovered, you might even become the very thing you despise."

"You got that right," said Aaronheim, "and because of that, I wholeheartedly share in the guilt. Really, if there was only something I could do…"

Mansford tapped his jaw. "Say, tell you what…. Maybe you could work for me. I'd say, that would be a decent start."

"Work for you?" Aaronheim scratched his head. "Sure…okay…but in what capacity?"

"I'm always in need of a good engineer," Mansford explained, "particularly one to oversee production. Isn't that right, Ned?"

"Absolutely," Stark concured, "especially when it comes to our more intricate products."

Aaronheim grinned. "Well, work is work, and at this point, I don't have anywhere else to go. Whatever I can do, Mister Mansford, I'm happy to oblige."

Mansford held out his hand. "Swell—it's a deal then. Ned will find you a room, and we'll negotiate your salary accordingly."

"Yes," said the scientist with a firm grasp, "it's a deal. It should prove a most interesting arrangement…but, uh, there's just one other thing."

Mansford raised an eyebrow.

"If I could get a pack of cigarettes anytime soon, I'd be most appreciative."

Mansford laughed. "There are plenty of corner stores in Brink Town. I'm sure we can oblige."

As the others took a moment to welcome Aaronheim aboard, Standish whispered to her man, "I'm so glad we broke free of that madness, and that you stood by me, Michael…well, to say the least, it means a lot." She fought back a tear, but followed it with a yawn. "I'm sorry, but I'm feeling rather drained." She leaned against him, closed her eyes. "Would it be all right if you took me home?"

"Yes, of course, dear," he said and glanced at her feet. "We'll even get you a nice, new pair of shoes tomorrow, a dress to match, okay? All will be right as rain." He then raised his voice for the others to hear. "I think we should all get back to our bases and get some well deserved rest."

As Poindexter and Charlie ushered everyone toward the limo, Clive leafed through his pad, scanning his notes.

Mansford and Standish moved past him, the former giving him a playful nudge. "Having a change of heart, Carl?"

"Heaven sakes, no," he laughed, but then looked serious. "I was thinking, though, that maybe I can still use this stuff. I mean, why not present it under the pretense of fiction, or perhaps hint that it may or may not be true? Readers can have fun deciding whatever they will."

"Not a bad idea, Mister Clive," said Charlie, opening the limo door. "Those dark avengers are all the rage today. Oh, there's nothing wrong with a good morality tale to get one in check. Heck, just last week I was reading the Phantom in your Sunday edition, and so inspired that…"

They let Charlie jabber on and entered the car, grateful to be alive, aligned, and pleased to be in the presence of their new recruit…

• • •

Mansford and Standish were the last to be dropped off, stopping at the night club to pick up his Packard.

For a short duration he sauntered about the structure's façade, recalling how for a moment, it had become a pseudo temple. How drab the place now looked in the light of day, but it only went to reason. All lies looked that way when exposed, and with that, he drove Standish home…

Once there, he crept with her upstairs and tucked her into bed. In spite of it all, she still looked innocent, her scent so pure and sincere, which led him to consider Montorto's claim that he put her at risk. He tossed the idea from his head, though, focusing instead on the day they would wed. They were meant to be together, no matter what the circumstance…

He headed back to his apartment, weary yet wide-eyed enough to stand at its open windows, absorbing the day's varying vibes, thinking of that unavoidable moment when again he would don his mask, fight the good fight, his faithful friends at his side.

EPILOGUE

The crumpled paper bounced like a tumbleweed across the dry grass: printed in Summer; though now it was Fall.

A tall, craggy entity approached it, and with its pale, stubby fingers snatched it up and read: NEW PERSONA ADVENTURE...BY CARL CLIVE...REAL OR IMAGINED...YOU DECIDE!

The entity emitted a froggy guffaw and sent the sheet back into the wind, shambling onward, until it reached a grassless patch.

It paused and then in boisterous German, it cried: "Rise, Herr Doktor. Rise from your niche."

The ground quaked, and a purple mist flowed between its grains until it presented the professor upon his back, his limbs stretched, surrounded by gnawed bones: big and small, human and simulated.

The professor opened his eyes, parted his green, blood-crusted lips. His nose twitched, catching the stench.

"I said, rise, Herr Doktor. Can you not hear? Do you not care? I have answered your prayers. I am here."

The thing unnerved Tarr and like a tense toddler, he sprung up and began to scurry away.

"What...what do you want?" he stammered. "Have you...have you come to judge me?"

"Judge you?" the shadowy shape asked. "Why would I judge you? That's not what you asked."

Tarr glanced at the bones. "I...I had no food," he explained. "It was either me or them. Even when I came across Good's men, I only fought out necessity, and then..."

The shape edged closer, its semblance growing more distinct under the noon's rays: two sets of legs and arms, with a man's head jutting through its neck, with two eyes distinct and another set beneath, sealed by a thin stretch of skin.

"I know," said the creature with feigned compassion. "I know."

Tarr relaxed and conjured the courage to ask, "So...so how did I get here?"

"You requested it," the creature replied, exasperated. "I heard your torturous plea: that is, at least once I found the means to crawl from out of my confinement." The creature paused and bowed pretentiously. "Please allow me to introduce myself." It smiled, revealing its sharp, crooked teeth. "I am Ben Gyler, but in the various underworld circles, I'm better known as the Great Beguiler." He

128

then straightened himself and with great political flair continued, "Among my kind, I am considered a king of kings, but from your research, you should know that. At any rate, it's a pleasure to meet you in the flesh, Herr Docktor, and I'm honored to accept your service under my command."

"Your…your command?" Tarr muttered. "What…what do you mean?"

"You are to work for me …help me find the means to break my physical torsion. Mansford—or rather his judgmental counterpart—twisted me into this horrid thing you now see. The alteration kept me shackled for quite some time and even recently prevented me from aiding my generals when they needed me most, in your strange, replicated dimension. Nevertheless, I have attempted to reshape myself ever since my fateful night of my defeat." The creature leaned into the light, revealing the gamut of its deformities. "Alas, as you can see, the results are hard to unravel."

Tarr cringed.

"Oh, don't be repulsed," the Beguiler said, shifting his eyes toward the bones. "After all, we each harbor our own form of ugliness."

"I…don't want any part of this," Tarr whimpered and turned away.

"Oh, but you will," said the Beguiler, "because you're as vindictive as I am. You also know that when our resources are combined, we can achieve heights neither of us could alone…particularly revenge." The Beguiler reached down, and raised Tarr's chin with its creepy, little fingers. "It's good to hold a grudge, Herr Doktor. If Mansford had only invested in your plan, there's no telling what you may have accomplished."

"No, I won't hear it," Tarr whined, but the creature's words rang far too true, cutting through what little was left of the professor's purity, sowing seeds of hate in his head.

"A pity," said the Beguiler. "I had so hoped to harness the elements around us and change what fate has dealt us." It shuffled backward, causing the soil to swirl like quicksand. "Ah, so be it, my good man. Perhaps it's just as well you return from whence you came."

Tarr trembled. He could not return to all that emptiness, all that despair, his stomach always growling, his mind always throbbing with animalistic intent.

"Wait," he said, reaching up. "Please, I beg of you…"

The swirling stopped, prompting the Guaner to dangle its hairy arms. "So," said the creature, "you've reconsidered." It grinned. "Gut, Herr Doktor, sehr gut."

The creature's affirmative tone stirred Tarr's mettle, and with a snap of his arm, he clasped the monster's hand, allowing the beast to pull him upward.

Coddling the professor within its sinewy upper limbs, the demon then turned toward the horizon.

"It's always good to start anew," the Great Beguiler croaked, "to set one's sights ever higher. Oh, fear not, Herr Doktor. Somehow, someway, the Persona will know the uncompromising power of our wrath. Your presence ensures that. In fact, my friend, you can bet your unconditional faith on it…"

THE END

ABOUT OUR CREATORS

AUTHOR -

MICHAEL HOUSEL - Over the years, has penned horror, science-fiction and psychodrama short stories, as well as reviews for toy and hobbyist periodicals. He is also the author of the monster-rally novel, "Flask of Eyes", published by Caliburn Press. You may visit his blog at http://bizarrechats.blogspot.com, where he offers reflections on a variety of fantasy-based topics.

INTERIOR ILLUSTRATIONS

KEVIN PAUL SHAW BRODEN, - initially seeking a career in comic books, took art courses throughout his education - only to eventually discover that no matter what the media, he was a storyteller at heart. Kevin received a BA in Art (emphasizing Narrative Illustration) from California State University, Fullerton (Fullerton, CA); before that, he worked on the HORNET newspaper as a reporter/illustrator while earning his AA at Fullerton College.

One of Kevin's early jobs teamed him with some of the talent that launched Supreme for Image Comics. You can even find a special "thank you" to Kevin in SUPREME #1. He storyboarded the music video for BiGod20's "One," as well as videos for John Wesley Harding and Kristin Hersch as part of Summer Arts in Humboldt, CA. Also, he's been contracted to do illustrations for commercials and television series pitches. The textbooks GARDNER'S GUIDE TO WRITING AND PRODUCING ANIMATION and GARDNER'S GUIDE TO PITCHING AND SELLING ANIMATION feature all interior art done by Kevin. With his wife and creative partner, Shannon Muir, Kevin created the online comic FLYING GLORY AND THE HOUNDS OF GLORY, which has been in existence over 15 years. His artwork has also been seen as the interior illustration for Ralph L. Angelo, Jr's "Against Fire and Stone" tale in LEGENDS OF NEW PULP FICTION by Airship 27 Productions, the cover art for the anthology NEWSHOUNDS from Pro Se Press (which also features his story "Stop the Presses!"), and as cover art for self-published e-books he's authored and released which include the REVENGE OF THE MASKED GHOST series and the CLOCKWORK GENIE MYSTERIES.

Oh, and yes, he does have FOUR NAMES. It's a family thing, but it comes in quite handy... FOUR NAMES OF PROFESSIONAL CREATIVITY.

COVER ARTIST

CHRIS RAWDING – is an eminent artist, educator and outdoor enthusiast. He has been a keen artist from his early days living on the South Shore of Massachusetts where he currently resides with his two sons. After attending the Museum School of Fine Arts and receiving his Bacherlor's in Commercial Illustration from the Art Institute of Boston, he now specializes in digital illustration, caricature design, branding and book illustration, as well as, screen printing and log design. His distinctive comic art style combined with his creativity and passion takes the subject matter to another level and uses color that don't exist in the real world, but makes them believable and turns them into edgy, eye-catching designs. As an eclectic visionary his gallery includes; pop culture, steampunk chic, superheroes and famous phantoms. For the past 20 years, he likes to take rish and pushes his concepts beyond the ordinary with a knack for modern, bold and organic design.

www.rawding.daportfolio.com

OCCULT DETECTIVES

They battle demons and monsters, hunt ghosts and defend us against the things that go bump in the night. They are Occult Detectives and they've been a staple of pulp fiction since the beginning of those glorious, garish magazines. Now Airship 27 Productions is thrilled to bring you a quartet of tales starring some of the most unique Occult Detectives ever created; three newly minted heroes and one classic master of mysticism.

From the days of the Wild West, Joel Jenkins offers up his Indian Shaman hero, Lone Crow. Then we have Josh Reynold's colorful Charles St. Cyprian, the Queen's own Royal Occultist, followed by Jim Beard's Sgt. Janus, the Spirit Breaker. And we culminate with a little known pulp classic figure, Ravenwood: the Stepson of Mystery as chronicled by Ron Fortier.

Get ready to take on possessed gunfighters, eerie mesmerizing spirits, a bewitching temptress and a legion of the undead as these four brand new tales usher you into thrilling adventures beyond the realm of the ordinary; your guides....the Occult Detectives.

PULP FICTION FOR A NEW GENERATION!

FOR AVAILABILITY INFORMATION: AIRSHIP27HANGAR.COM